NORTEX PRESS NORTEX Waco, Texas

Stories in this volume were originally published in the following venues:

"The Copper Bell" in *The North American Review.*
"Miriam's Story" in *Haunted Voices, Haunting Places: An Anthology of Writers of the Old and New South* (Halcyon Press, 2008).
"The Skinny-dippers" in *New Texas: A Journal of Literature and Culture.*
"Covered Bridge Road" in *Carpe Articulum Literary Review.*

The author wishes to express his gratitude to Southern Arkansas University for a Research Fellowship that allowed him to complete work on this manuscript.

COVER ART: Rene Magritte, *L'empire des lumieres (The Dominion of Light)*. The Menil Collection, Houston. Photograph by George Hixson, 1996.

Produced for Halcyon Press

FIRST EDITION

Printed in the United States of America
By Nortex Press—A Division of Sunbelt Media, Inc.
P.O. Box 21235 Waco, Texas 76702
email: sales@eakinpress.com
website: www.eakinpress.com

1 2 3 4 5 6 7 8 9
ISBN 13: 978-1-935632-32-0
ISBN 10: 1-935632-32-9
Library of Congress Control Number 2012941338

Contents

Foreword

There are two kinds of ghosts in the modern ghost story. One is those who literally walk around and rattle their chains, as in Dickens. The other is those who are mere projections of the protagonist's mind, as in Elizabeth Bowen. James Ulmer's ghosts are of the latter variety, what Edmund Wilson called probings of "psychological caverns where the contents of that life have engendered disquieting obsessions" (*Classics and Commercials: A Literary Chronicle of the Forties*. New York: Farrar, Straus & Company, p. 175). Ulmer is aware of the distinction. In "Miriam's Story" he writes, "He wanted Henry James, and he was afraid he was about to get Poe." In that story, the possibility of other ghosts in the restaurant is tantalizing. One might possibly be D. H. Lawrence.

Ulmer's stories like "The Copper Bell" are written in rich poetic language, which should not surprise, since he is also a poet. That story displays excellent child psychology about what one does not know or comprehend. In "The Orchard Road" the author gives us fine nature descriptions. "The Blue Garden" is evocative and subtle. Ulmer makes allusions to Tolstoy, Dante, Rilke, Lawrence, Irving, and Frost. I'd also suggest there is an influence of Hawthorne's characters who actively seek ecstatic experience.

Attention should be paid to Ulmer's use of symbolism, such as the jerking scarecrow and the distorted reflections in hand-blown glass.

In many of these stories an individual seeks to give expression to the life before this one. "The Emissary" is one example. This is not to say there is a sameness to the stories. In "Covered Bridge Road," for example, a childhood favorite place is as much a ghost as a childhood friend. "Uncle Edward" is highly original and unfolds cinematically. It and "The Skinny-dippers" and "The Tea Roses" are my favorites in the collection. Ulmer is at his best in the longer stories, particularly "The Tea Roses." Doubtless he admires James' "blest nouvelle."

Another quality worth noting in these tales is how consistently they examine the imaginative process. Indeed, it is this process that often serves to introduce the element of mystery or transcendence in the piece. In Ulmer's work, making art opens doors. Painters, for example, serve as protagonists in four of these tales ("Covered Bridge Road," "The Emissary," "In the Butterfly House," and "Uncle Edward"), and the narrator in "The Tea Roses" is a writer. In addition, the first two stories in this collection could accurately be described as stories about the effects of telling stories.

Why would anyone read (or write) ghost stories in the age of the computer? To quote Edmund Wilson again, there are two reasons. The first is "a longing for mystic experience which seems always to manifest itself in periods of social confusion . . . as soon as we feel that our world has failed us, we try to find evidence for another world." The second reason is "the instinct to inoculate ourselves against panic at the real horrors loose on the earth." As examples he mentions the Gestapo and airplane bombings (Wilson, p. 173). James Ulmer's volume is a valuable addition to this literary milieu.

—Robert Phillips
The University of Houston

"And what is there? and who is there?
there, beyond that field and that tree,
and the roofs with the sunlight on them?"

—Leo Tolstoy

The Copper Bell

He tried not to think about what had happened that day. He was not ready to think about that yet. So instead, he pictured her hands as he lay under the blankets and the watery darkness swam around the room. If her hands were not cradling a book, then more than likely they would be powdered with flour. The first time he had walked into the kitchen and seen her white hands he'd been frightened; but then he had realized it was only the flour, and his nose had registered the billowing scent of hot apples and cinnamon. This is how he remembered her: either baking in the kitchen in her blue, flour-dusted apron, making bread rise or pies appear from scratch from whatever fruit the season offered, or holding a book as she told him one of her stories.

And it came to him then in a flurry of wings—how she'd always fed the birds! He saw her in his mind scattering bread crumbs on the frozen ground to chickadees in their black mufflers who pecked and cheeped and seemed to arrive from everywhere out of the cold, brilliant morning. A cardinal descended like flame to perch on the icy clothesline just above her head as the wind blew open her dark green coat. When she came in to where he'd watched, peering over the sill of the dining room window, her clothes and face had smelled like cold air.

Hearing a noise, he sat up in bed and listened. But it was only the creak of the floor or the wooden staircase, a sound the empty darkness sometimes makes. She'd told him that. It was a few years ago when he was very young, only four, and still terrified of being alone in the dark.

She had told him then that what we think is out in the darkness, in the closet or lurking in the corner shadow, is something inside us and really not there at all. He was not sure he understood completely—is a thing not there simply because it is inside us?—but he had felt his terror subside a little when she'd said it. And then she had given him the copper bell engraved with stars. She had told him that if he needed her, he could ring the bell and she would hear it in the night and come. She showed him how to ring it, holding it by the top in her thumb and first finger and shaking it lightly back and forth. He had never used the bell, but he was always comforted to see it standing ready on the night table; and on some nights, when the wind howled and rattled at his window and the moon cast long shadows in the room, he had gone to sleep with the bell clutched in his palm.

Last Christmas, she had lingered at the table with her sisters, empty dessert plates and china cups in front of them, and the talk had begun. He had listened from the other room—how their brother Karl, who'd died at a place called Dachau, had gone out at night when he was a boy to the grave of a rich man's son who had died mysteriously. The three sisters and their husbands leaned together and lowered their voices as the story continued, lapsing into speech he could not understand, the words chugging like a train through a string of harsh consonants, questions and answers moving back and forth across the table, so it was only by the tone of their voices that he'd had any idea what they said. He had to finish the story for himself: Karl walking back to town along the railroad tracks, something unseen walking with him—all the way back inside the stone walls of the old city, to the house where their father kept a butcher's shop . . .

He loved the stories she had told him. He would wait, like now, and she would enter with her book and open it in the light spilling from his bedside lamp. She always opened to the story she wanted to tell, and though she turned the pages as she went and even ran one finger lightly down the glossy page as if she could feel the letters, she never glanced at the words. She told each story by heart, her eyes on his eyes, her face changing as the story changed, her voice low—a whisper thick with her accent—as if a secret were passing between them. *A soldier was returning home from the wars. On the road home he met an old witch who tied a rope around his waist and lowered him through a hollow oak into underground rooms full of treasure. All the witch wanted was a tinderbox, a small thing no bigger than this*—and she pointed to the bell on the night stand. *The soldier filled his pockets and boots with coins, found the witch's tinderbox, and slowly, she pulled him up toward the light at the top of the tree. He could see it all as if he were there, could see the circle of light growing larger as he rose toward it out of the darkness.* She told him how the soldier, at the top of the stairs in his lonely garret room, discovered the secret of the tinderbox. *And the dogs were summoned, brought gold, brought the princess, sleeping, on their backs.*

Although he could not have put the thought into words, he understood that the stories were about awakenings, and sometimes about going so deeply to sleep that waking could begin a new life. He remembered so much: Pinocchio growing donkey ears on Pleasure Island; the beautiful white rose that Beauty's father picked in the garden at night, making Beast rise up from the shadows; a house made of gingerbread hiding its lurking threat. And the poison apple, one half white and one half red, and how Snow-White was tricked into tasting it. *So the seven little men came home to find her dead on the floor. They washed her body with wine and water and laid her in a coffin of glass. An owl, a raven, and a dove perched on the coffin to mourn her, and one day the king's son rode deep into the forest, and he saw her and loved her. . . . When he picked up the coffin the piece of apple fell out of her throat, and she sat up and opened her eyes.*

Down the hall, he could sense his mother and father sleeping in the darkness, worn out after a day of tears. Why couldn't he sleep? The swirling moonlight kept his thoughts turning. A breeze stepped in through the window and ran across the floor, shaking out its cold, fragrant hair. He was expectant, waiting for something. At the cemetery that day, he'd peered over the wall of flowers with their sweet, dizzying tangle of odors to watch as her coffin was lowered into the ground. He could smell the earth, and for an instant, the lid of the coffin had turned to glass. She had opened her eyes then and looked at him with the same silent promise he'd seen so often before when she sat on the edge of his bed, the open book in her lap, pausing before she began to lisp the syllables of her tale. Everyone told him that she was dead, but what did that mean? Children know—deeply, instinctively—that death is not the end of anything, since it is not the end of what they feel. Later, their house had been full of grown-ups he hardly knew. He'd endured their sad eyes on him and their strange hands patting his head as he sat silently on the bottom of the staircase. He had blocked out the legs milling around him, the well-intentioned words that meant nothing to him, and clutched to himself his marvelous secret: the look that had passed between them!

He turned then and saw the curved shape of the bell in the darkness. Sitting up, he reached out and took it in his hand. It was cold to the touch, and he ran his fingers over the etched dispersal of stars, a galaxy to fit in his palm. He only paused for a moment, then grasped it by the top and shook it as she had done. The bell emitted a high, silvery shiver of notes, delicate but piercing, sounding as if it would carry for a long, long way through the silence.

He lay back down then, listening carefully, minutely, but at last closed his eyes and drifted off.

THE MOON HAD SET, and he listened in a darkness so complete it felt as if he'd fallen to the bottom of a deep well. Was he awake now or asleep? It hardly mattered. Someone was coming up the stairs, the steps soft but deliberate. He waited for the doorknob to rotate, for the door to open a crack and the white fingers to curl around the jamb, for the steps to approach across the floor. She would switch on the lamp, and the light would spill over the book she carried. Her fingers would touch the words as she spoke.

He knew, then, that there would always be more stories.

Miriam's Story

They entered because the rain was ferocious and the glow of the windows had drawn them in the dark. Standing in the entrance, Jon shook the weather from his umbrella and glanced around the café. It was nearly deserted, only one other couple and a single reader lingering over his coffee and book at a corner table. The leaded glass windows reflected the light of a fire crackling at the far end of the room; without a word, they headed for the empty table near the hearth. The storm that had caught them off guard had been ushered into town by a blue norther that had dropped the temperature more than twenty degrees in half an hour, not an unusual occurrence in that Gulf coast city in winter. Despite the umbrella Jon always carried in his car, they were both drenched, and the fire was a welcome and unexpected comfort.

So they settled in, Miriam with her back to the fire. She kept her eyes averted, the faint smile Jon found so difficult to interpret edging her mouth. Was it irony? If so, at whose expense? At last, she looked up and met his gaze.

"So, what did you think of the artist?" she asked. Rain had blurred slightly the mascara rimming her dark eyes.

"What did you think?" he countered.

"Do you always answer a question with a question?"

Jon was fairly certain that she already knew what he thought. But as usual, she seemed determined to unsettle him, to tip awry his comfortable balance, and he savored the slight vertigo he always felt in her presence. They had gone that evening to see a performance artist. He despised performance art. Take someone with no significant talent in any art form, combine those art forms, and add a lot of nerve and a morbid desire for attention, and the result was a performance artist. But it was a chance to spend a night with Miriam, so he had willingly sat next to her, close enough to feel her heat and smell her hair, while a woman on stage wearing only panties had splashed paint on her body in the cold, blue flash of a strobe light, and then had proceeded to smear that paint on an otherwise perfectly good stretch of white canvas, all the while reciting Anne Sexton's "In Celebration of My Uterus." It had been deeply silly and pretentious; but the truth was, Jon would've gladly attended a picnic in an outhouse in the middle of July if Miriam were going to be present. She had him enthralled. He knew it, and he was afraid that she knew it, too.

A waiter approached, and he ordered an old bottle of Rioja, as well as some baked brie and chorizo to bring out the flavor of the wine.

"Didn't you like the poem?"

"Sure," Jon responded when the waiter had stepped away. "But I could've done without the bimbo. Anne Sexton deserves better."

She leaned toward him, teasing him with her eyes. "Didn't you think the artist had pretty breasts?"

"I've seen better." Jon smiled at her to sure she understood the compliment.

"But the paint," Miriam persisted, "the blue light, the texture of the artist's body and the texture of the canvas." She was nearly singing, and her eyes were so dark in the dim light that they seemed all pupil, ecstatic. "Aren't you interested in new ways of feeling? In new combinations of sensations?"

"Of course."

He was—especially with her. He remembered the Halloween party where they'd met. A dozen female vampires had stalked the alcohol-soaked gathering that night, but Miriam had been, in his eyes, the undisputed queen. Auburn hair so dark it was almost black, cut short and spiked on top. What would've been butch on another woman was devastatingly feminine on her. A man with long green legs wearing a jar that read *Sweet Basil* had asked her to dance, and when she'd spun out onto the floor her black gown had flared out, revealing legs so pale, so flawless, that Jon had thought, at first, that she was wearing body paint. She'd caught him staring and seemed entertained by his embarrassment. He had to admit it: she'd picked him out. She had been so beautiful, so dangerously perfect, that he wasn't certain he would've had the cold nerve to approach her. And later, after the moon had set and the boozy caterwaul of the party had been abandoned, Jon had followed her giddily up the narrow stairs to her apartment. She'd danced just out of reach a few steps ahead of him, laughing, beckoning with a single slim finger, the nail painted black. What an exquisite surprise it had been to discover that the pale young woman in black was not marble after all, but warm, breathing flesh.

That had been over six weeks ago, and Jon had repeated the experience as often as she would permit it. Old friends had started to call and leave messages on his voice-mail, worried that they never saw him anymore. In a sense, he'd been kidnapped, but he was a willing victim.

The waiter returned with their wine and two long-stemmed glass balloons and began to go through the ritual. He displayed the label, and when Jon nodded his approval, the waiter deftly cut away the lead from the mouth of the bottle, twisted in the corkscrew, and, as silently as possible, drew out the cork. This was a sacrament Jon enjoyed: the anticipation lent particular savor to the first taste of the wine. The waiter splashed a half-inch of the rose-colored liquid into Jon's glass and stood back. Jon raised the glass, swirled the wine, and held the goblet under his nose to breathe in the scent of fruit and wood; then he tipped up the glass and held the wine in his mouth for a moment before swallowing.

Crushed cherries and vanilla, a woodsy, floral quality that was familiar somehow but difficult to pin down.

"Well, Professor Clarke, does the wine meet with your approval?"

Jon taught English, or tried to, at the local community college, and Miriam always used his title with mild derision. Again he confronted her smile.

"Yes, it does." He looked up at the waiter. "It's very good." The waiter thanked him politely and filled both balloons halfway before withdrawing. Jon and Miriam clicked glasses and drank.

"It *is* good," she agreed, making peace. She returned her glass to the table but left her hand on the stem: white fingers, black nails, the glowing garnet wine.

Above them her eyes, dark and predatory, watching him.

THE RAIN CONTINUED TO FALL, tapping steadily on the roof and running in streams down the windows, blotting out the outside world. The headlights of a passing car swept one window, casting a pattern of streaks and drops briefly across the wall.

"What a night," Jon commented, shivering for a moment, his clothes still damp. "Good night for a ghost story."

She took him up at once. "Do you believe in ghosts?"

"Not really," he admitted. "I'm an agnostic, I guess. The idea is intriguing, but it's hard for me to believe without some kind of evidence. Or a personal experience, at least."

Miriam leaned toward him, her eyes widening. "So you've never seen a ghost?"

She was teasing, leading him on—he wasn't sure where—and he momentarily rebelled. "No, I haven't. My experience with spirits is limited to the kind found in this glass. The scariest thing I've seen lately was that performance artist."

She refused the bait. Instead, she deliberately paused, took a mouthful of the wine, and held it for a moment before swallowing. "How do you know you've never seen one?"

"I think I'd know, don't you?"

"No. I don't think you would." She smiled her faint smile. "I have a theory about this. I think the dead are all around us, all the time. We walk right past them on the street, lost in our own thoughts and petty problems—something our boss said, how we're going to pay our light bill—and we don't recognize them. We don't see them or what their presence means. They don't fit in with our sense of things, and you can't see what you don't believe is there."

Jon listened to the storm, considering. It was a strange idea, odd but compelling, typical of her. "Have *you* ever seen a ghost?" he asked.

It was difficult to pose that question with a straight face, especially with the rain drumming and, just now, a distant rumbling crash of thunder. He felt as if he were on the set of a bad horror movie. It was all so unlikely, so melodramatic. He wanted Henry James, and he was afraid he was about to get Poe. But Jon sensed that she had a story to tell, so he tried to keep his doubts from showing. He wanted to hear it.

"I WAS FOURTEEN, and it was New Year's Eve. I was babysitting for some of the local rich folks. They had this old house that had been the center of a huge farm before the suburbs I lived in were built up around it."

Eyes downcast, the wine in its long-stemmed glass held like a rose in her pale hand.

"Was it a creepy old place?"

"No, sorry," she said, looking up at him with a weight in her eyes, refusing his irony. "In fact, it was a real showplace. Hand-hewn pine floors, crown moldings, a marble fireplace. The original chandelier from before the Civil War hung over the table in the formal dining room, and every October, the Wiltons—that was their name—used to let the county historical society conduct guided tours of the house. And there were no weird stories about the place, either—at least none that I'd ever heard. Mrs. Wilton had put the baby to bed, and they went off to some costume party. I remember she was dressed like Scarlett O'Hara. A dark green silk dress, off the shoulders, a hooped skirt. I was *so* jealous," she smiled. "I wanted that dress."

"You would've been beautiful in it." He meant it. He was picturing every word she said.

Miriam tipped her head curtly, acknowledging the compliment, then drained the last of her wine. He filled her glass again and topped his own.

"The baby slept all night, so I stayed downstairs drinking the soda they'd left in the frig and reading."

"Reading what?" he wanted to know.

"Nothing scary, if that's what you mean. I studied my algebra for a while—I was doing terrible in Math—and when that got old, I found a copy of *Lady Chatterley's Lover* on the Wiltons' bookshelf."

Jon was surprised. "I had no idea you were so literary as a teenager."

"I wasn't. I'd heard it was a dirty book, and I was curious."

"Yeah, he's filthy." Lawrence was one of Jon's favorite writers. "People opening like flowers. Souls like twin stars balancing each other in the firmament. Nasty stuff."

"What did I know?" Miriam shrugged. "I was fourteen. I was paging through the book, looking for the sex. I was at the part where the gamekeeper takes Lady Chatterley to see the pheasants hatching—I remember this so clearly—and I looked up and saw a man standing just inside the front door. The foyer wasn't lit, so I thought at first my eyes were playing tricks on me, but when I looked more closely, there he was: standing in the shadows, watching me. He never said a word."

Jon's uneasiness crept up on him. "What was he doing there?"

"He was waiting for me to notice him. I stared into the shadows, and I saw him more clearly with every second that passed. He had dark hair, swept back as if the wind had done it, and a pair of knee-high black boots, a gray cloak over his shoulders. His boots were splattered with mud, and I remember thinking that he must've ridden for a long, long way." Her white hand traveled to the stem of her glass. "He had a riding crop in one hand," she added, her eyes hard, fixed in memory, "and he wore a mask."

A log popped loudly in the fireplace behind her. Jon flinched. "What kind of mask?"

"A black mask over his eyes, with sequins at the pointed corners, like a Mardi Gras mask."

As she responded, Miriam's fingers drew the mask over her own eyes, and for an instant, it seemed to appear on her face in the dim, rain-flecked air. She had lowered her voice nearly to a whisper, causing him to lean unconsciously closer—she was singing, calling out like a Lorelei to something submerged in him, using her voice and her eyes to put a different world in the place of his own. He saw what she was doing: he saw. She was damn good at it. Their food arrived, rescuing him, and he gave himself over to the sausage and the smooth, delicate cheese, grateful to escape for a moment the tightening noose of her words. Jon encouraged her to eat as well, but Miriam sat quietly, waiting, apparently confident of her advantage, not needing to push it.

He cut a slice of brie and smeared it on a crust of bread. *Get a hold of yourself*, he fumed. He signaled to the waiter and ordered a second bottle. For the space of a few minutes, Jon ate in silence, and neither of them spoke.

BUT THERE WAS MORE to her story: there had to be. She was allowing him to concede, to admit defeat, but he couldn't do that. For one thing, he needed to know what had happened.

So, after the waiter had delivered the wine and withdrawn, Jon topped his glass again and, smiling coolly, filled hers, as well. *Give me your best shot*, he thought.

"Weren't you afraid?"

"When?" Miriam asked.

Nice touch. So innocent. She stared at him with her blank, black eyes.

"When you saw that man in the shadows," he prompted her. "Weren't you afraid?"

"Of course. For one thing, he'd startled me. I hadn't heard the door open, you know? And it was a little unnerving because he was looking at me so intently. Has anyone ever done that to you—*stared* at you, and when you notice, you realize he's been doing it for a while, watching every gesture, every expression? Well, it was creepy, intrusive. He wanted something, but at the time I had no idea what it was. He stepped forward, moving out of the shadows by the door, and his eyes behind that black mask never left me. Then I *was* frightened. He was as close to me as that wall." Jon turned to where she'd indicated: an inside brick wall fifteen or twenty paces away. "But then I thought it must be Mr. Wilton. When I'd arrived at the house earlier, he'd already gone around back to get the car, so I hadn't seen his costume. This man was the same size and build as Wilton. I figured it had to be him. He must've forgotten something and come back for it.

Then, as if he knew what I was thinking, the man lifted the mask and put it on his forehead. He was definitely *not* Terence Wilton."

Jon felt a thrill climb his spine. "Who was he?" He caught himself whispering, entering her register.

"I have no idea. I'd never seen him before, and I've never seen him since. He just stood there, looking at me, smiling this knowing smile." The identical smile curled at Miriam's lips, and he felt disoriented for a moment, unsure of where he was.

"He wanted me to see him," she added.

"What makes you think so?" Jon swirled his wine and took a greedy mouthful, trying to regain his equilibrium.

"They want to be seen."

"They?"

He knew damn well what she meant, but he wanted her to say it.

"A living man would've spoken," Miriam replied. "But he was still, as if he stood in an envelope of silence. Then he bowed from the waist, turned to his right, and walked up the stairs. And get this"—she reached across the table and touched Jon's hand, and he felt the hair rise in a cold wave over his arm—"those stairs were wooden and uncarpeted, and the big black boots he had on never made a sound when he walked up them! Not so much as a creak."

"Strange story." He tried to sound casual.

"There's more." Her eyes flashed wickedly, and Jon thought for the twentieth time that night how beautiful she was. "The baby was upstairs, remember?"

ENOUGH REMAINED in the second bottle for a last glass apiece. Jon lifted the bottle and looked at her inquiringly, and when she nodded, he divided the wine between them. Miriam raised her glass to drink, and he noted how dark her lips were, several shades redder than the wine. Her mouth left no smear of lipstick on the rim.

"How do you know it wasn't one of Wilton's friends? Maybe they got drunk at their costume party and decided to play a trick on the babysitter."

She shook her head. "Not possible. I was reading. The television wasn't on. He would've had to unlock the door, open it, and lock it again behind him. The front door of that house made a sound like a dungeon gate when it opened. I never heard a thing."

"Maybe Wilton left the door open. Put some tape over the latch so his friend could just slip in."

Jon was feeling confident, fighting back successfully now with his common sense.

"When that man went upstairs," she countered, "I ran to the front door to check it. It was locked up tight. Then I stood at the bottom of the staircase, listening. Earlier that evening, I'd gone upstairs with Mrs. Wilton to look in on the baby. A hallway ran the length of the house, and those pine floorboards were old and a little warped. They gave slightly and creaked when you stepped on them. There was no place he could've gone but down that hall, but it was silent as an empty church. Not a sound."

Jon was silent, as well. He'd run out of explanations, and he felt the force of her story stealing over him again. The odd thing was, he didn't believe it: not a word of it. But it worked on him, anyway.

Seeing her advantage, Miriam pressed on.

"The baby was upstairs—still sleeping, thank goodness—and that man, or whatever he was, had gone up there. I didn't think he'd hurt the child. Somehow, I knew his business was with me. But I had to check. The last thing in the world I wanted to do was go up those stairs, but I had no choice. I was supposed to be watching the baby, you know? So I got a carving knife from the kitchen, and I held it in front of me with both hands, trying to keep from shaking. I went up that creaky old staircase a step at a time, cringing at the noise I was making, expecting my mystery man to appear at any instant from around the corner at the top of the stairs."

The waiter walked past their table and poked at the dying fire. A storm of sparks rose in a stream up the flu, and a single tongue of flame appeared to lick again at the charred wood. Jon tipped up his glass and drained the last of his wine, down to the muddy grains.

"What were you expecting to do with that knife?" he asked.

"Beats me. You can't kill the dead." Miriam grinned. "It's too late."

"So, did he jump out at you?"

"No." The smile vanished. "I guess that's the strangest part. In a way, it would've been easier to take if he had—if it had turned out to be some kind of stupid joke. The baby's room was the first one on the left, the door ajar so I could hear her if she woke up and started to cry. I can still see it. Some blue from the nightlight drifted into the hall. It looked like snow." She was there again. From across the table, Miriam fixed him with her eyes. "No one in the room. I checked the closet, too, of course. Then I bundled up the baby as quietly as I could, took her downstairs, and put her on the couch. I went back upstairs, that silly knife shaking in my hands, and I searched every room. I left the doors open as I went and kept an eye on the hall so he couldn't slip past me. Each time I threw open a closet door, my heart was racing so fast I thought I was going to faint. All the rooms were empty."

"Maybe there was another way downstairs or outside."

Miriam shook her head slowly from side to side. "This was a Georgian house. Everything symmetrical, at right angles. There was nowhere you could've concealed a back stair or a hidden passage. I checked every door and window in the house, and they were all locked from the inside. I was terrified, cold all over. I couldn't stop shaking. Not because he was in the house—the place was empty, I could feel it—but because he wasn't. There was no way he could've gotten into the house, and once in, there was no way he could've gotten out."

"But you saw him."

"As plainly as you see me."

"What did you do?"

Again her sibyl's smile. "I died of fright."

THEY REGARDED EACH OTHER in silence across the table.

"How did the Wiltons take it?" Jon asked. "Did you tell them?"

She smiled sardonically. "I was never invited back."

He searched his mind, looking for the right denial, the phrase that would dissipate the spell she'd woven. But before he could find it, she spoke.

"The dead are all around us, Jon. If we could see them, if we knew they were there, our world would be changed forever."

The waiter brought their bill. Jon signed the credit card receipt and left a tip, and they rose to go. Looking around the café, he noticed that the place was empty. The other customers had slipped away, but he'd been so rapt, so caught up in her story, that he'd never seen them leave. How had she managed that? Part of him realized that she'd most likely made the whole thing up—but then he thought of the sounds the old house emitted and the blue glow of the nightlight drifting like snow. She'd made it real. They stood together in the doorway, looking out, reluctant to leave the warmth of the café and its dying fire. The rain was still falling, but softly now, putting a shine on the walkway and on the blackened road, and wet steel gleamed on the cars parked along the curb. Even the air had been transformed, and Jon inhaled the unfamiliar cold with its trace of the arctic, as if an iceberg, something massive, loomed behind the water-darkened houses.

He opened his umbrella as they stepped out into the night, and Miriam pressed close to him and put her arm around his waist. He angled the umbrella to cover her as well as he could and shortened his stride to match hers. He felt lonely in his skin, and he thought of her white body on the black satin sheets of her bed and of the oils she used that warmed to the touch.

She had him; she'd won. Well, he had wanted her to all along.

A man lumbered past, shoulders hunched, forming suddenly out of the depths of the rain.

Jon was startled by the quick appearance and watched with relief as the man receded and vanished into the night. When he turned to Miriam, her dark eyes were only inches from his, the two of them insulated under his umbrella from the fine, needling rain.

"But how do you know he wasn't?" she whispered, reading him. "How can you be sure?"

The Orchard Road

"But I am done with apple picking now..."

The summer after I graduated from college, I stayed on in that town of nineteenth-century brick row houses. My friends returned to the affluent suburban neighborhoods of New York, Philadelphia, or Washington that they'd all come from, turning their bright and expensively educated faces toward the future; but not me. For the first time in my life, I was aware of something good ending never to return, of time flowing past, sweeping away everything in its path, and I was determined not to lose the connection I felt I'd found. There was something there for me; maybe it was the proximity of the past, some energy left from all the soldiers, Union and Confederate alike, who lay buried in the fields nudging up against those old houses—some little piece of eternity I thought I'd lose forever if I left.

For a while, my girlfriend, Allison, stayed with me. We took a one-room apartment a few blocks from campus and moved in with the mattress I threw on the floor, some cheap dishes from the local thrift shop, and my dog-eared paperback copies of Melville and Faulkner. My intention was to spend time listening to the great voices of the living dead. For money, I drove a tour bus on the Civil War battlefield, timing my drive to coincide with the recording that played through a set of speakers mounted in the back of the bus. The battlefield, a national park, surrounded the town on three sides, sealing it in a kind of bubble, protecting it from the encroachment of strip malls and condominiums.

Allison had long red hair and a flower tattoo on one ankle. She wrote bad poetry and listened, almost continually, to records by The Allman Brothers Band and The Grateful Dead. She was the only woman I'd known, at that point in my life, who was willing to have sex with me pretty much whenever I wanted, and being young, I mistook her pliancy for devotion. One evening, I looked up from *Walden* to find Allison's green eyes, heavy with an unspoken question, fixed on me.

"What is it?" I asked.

"You seem content," she observed, her eyes flicking dismissively around our squalid Bohemian digs. "Don't you want more than this?"

"Not really," I shrugged.

Too abstracted to be alarmed, I was, instead, amused; my hippie girlfriend was getting ambitious—ambitious for me, of all things. The truth is, I was terribly ambitious—enmeshed like Thoreau in a great experiment—but not in a way that was likely to get us decent furniture. Frowning pensively, Allison wandered away to run a bath.

When I arrived home from work a few days later, I was shocked to discover that she'd packed up and left. It was mid-August by then, that part of the summer when the goldenrod hangs heavy in the fields and the first nuance of autumn makes its presence felt. I found a note telling me that she'd gone back to New Jersey. She'd taken with her the potted geranium we'd coaxed to life on the fire escape.

Summer came slowly to a close. After Labor Day, the steady flow of tourists to the battlefield began to drop off, and I lost my job. Determined not to give up, not to lose the thing I was groping for so blindly, I quickly found a new job at the Musselman's plant in Biglerville, a few miles outside town.

Every morning at six-fifteen, I left my solitary apartment and drove into the country in my faded blue 1968 Volkswagen Beetle, the crack in the windshield on the passenger's side breaking the landscape into Cubist planes. I'd roll down the window to feel the coolness and smell the dew from the fields and the old trees with rags of mist around their roots. Almost invariably, as I turned off the main road into the network of winding farm lanes that took me to the plant, my sputtering motor would scare up a pheasant or a brace of woodcocks from the roadside; and sometimes, I'd spot a raccoon ambling back into the trees after a night of foraging. I always took these brief encounters as omens, as if I were getting a glimpse of some secret life, though what precisely was being foretold I could never determine. But I felt that if I kept watching, that if I was patient and remembered everything I saw, then the pieces would come together and some startling mystery would be revealed.

My job at Musselman's was to assist Tom McAdams. Tom was five years older than me, the son of one of the local apple growers. He had a ponytail, a beard, and a small silver hoop in his left ear; he also had a wealth of local legend at his disposal and a business on the side selling furniture made from apple wood. In my eyes, Tom was the ideal combination of Jerry Garcia and Johnny Appleseed. He drove a flatbed truck with four-wheel drive and a power gate on the back, and our task was to make the rounds of the orchards mapping the hillsides and pick up the crates of apples left by crews of migrant pickers. Tom would maneuver his truck down the rutted dirt lanes between the rows of apple trees, getting as close as he could to the crate; then he'd lower the power gate and we'd shove our prize onto the flatbed. Weighed down with stacked crates of Rome beauties, Mackintoshes, and Granny Smiths, as well as the huge red Eisenhower apples that would sell for fifty cents apiece, we'd head back to the plant and unload the fruit, where it would be cleaned, sorted, and sent to a distribution center in York.

Tom hadn't gone to college, and he was determined to teach me, the smart-ass college kid, something I didn't already know. That was fine with me. I'd never been adverse to the idea that there were things to learn outside of books.

"You know," he began, eyeing me sideways one afternoon, "these old women who've lived out here on these farms all their lives—they know shit, man."

We were parked in the shade at the far end of an orchard, out of sight of the farmhouse, our flatbed loaded with crates. Tom passed me the joint he'd lit.

"Like what?" I took a hit and squinted at him through the rising smoke.

"Well, take my great-aunt Peg, for instance. She's seventy-six years old, and she lives in the same house she was born in, the house her grandfather built in 1872. She knows this land like the sight of her own shadow. That woman's never been to a pharmacist in her life. If she has a headache, or she can't sleep—or, when she was younger, if she wanted to get pregnant or *didn't* want to get pregnant—out she goes into the meadow and finds the plant or flower she needs. I've seen her do it, man. She's *always* making tea out of something."

Maybe it was the grass, but I was intrigued. Silently, I passed the joint back to him.

"She's a witch," I suggested.

Tom glanced at me quickly to make sure I wasn't insulting his family, and when he saw I wasn't, he took a long pull on the reefer, releasing, after a moment, a cloud of blue smoke that billowed meditatively around his temples.

"Yeah," he replied. "I guess you could say she is. Know what she told me one time? When she was girl, her mother told her that if she stood in front of a mirror at midnight when there was a full moon, she'd see the face of her future husband appear at her shoulder. So she did it, and she saw the face."

Tom shot me a grave look, as if he were daring me to laugh,

then passed me the last of the joint. I pinched it carefully from between his thumb and first finger.

"The next day," he continued, exhaling, "she went into town and met the train. She just stood there in the station, in her best dress and a wide-brimmed straw hat, looking at the men who stepped off the platform, city boys mostly, until she saw the face from the mirror."

I sucked up the last of the smoke before pitching the roach out the truck window. It arced through the green shadows and landed in the orchard grass, where it glowed for a moment before going out.

Tom touched me on the forearm for emphasis. "She walked up to him, only fifteen years old, and told him he was the man she was gonna marry. He was from Harrisburg, almost twice her age, and had a job as a traveling salesman. The man never batted an eye. She took him home, and two days later, they were hitched. That was my great-uncle Harry. He lived with her in that old house for fifty-five years, until he died, and never so much as wandered past the edge of the property."

I looked at him distrustfully.

"True story, man," he insisted.

"How'd she manage that?"

Tom shrugged. "Nobody knows."

Afternoon shadows played across the hood of the truck. The THC hit my bloodstream, and I felt that sense of drawing partly out of myself.

"Is your great-aunt Peg still alive?"

"Sure is. Want to meet her some time?"

I did. I was curious about the woman who knew the properties of every weed and flower in those fields, a woman who could hold a man, a stranger to her, in thrall for over half a century.

Tom turned over the engine, and we headed back to the plant, the two of us as high as windblown kites. We unloaded at the back dock our crates of fruit, green and golden and every imaginable shade of red, stem end and blossom end. A few stubborn yellow jackets hovered over the bruised, cidery rejects in the trash barrel. I felt like the narrator in the Frost poem, the one who dreams of apples as the long winter sleep comes on.

WORK KEPT ME BUSY for a while. At night, back in town, I'd haunt the bar on the square that had been my hangout for the previous four years, but the new crop of coeds, though I plied them with shots and beers, wanted nothing to do with a guy they perceived as a townie. It was disconcerting to realize how quickly I'd lost my place in the social order. The previous year, I'd been a senior, desirable and mature, a young man on the verge. Now I was nothing, and the world had passed me by.

One sunny, cold afternoon in mid November, Tom drove the winding, unmarked maze of farm roads through fields of harvested corn. The dry stalks bent and rustled their papery leaves in the north wind. He turned off on a dirt lane and rattled through a stand of pines, pulling up in front of an old white house hidden from the road. A scarecrow impaled on a stake twisted in the wind above a patch of kitchen garden, the wide-brimmed black hat pulled low over his stitched and painted face.

But there was no orchard, no crates of apples to retrieve.

"What's this?" I asked.

From behind the wheel, Tom aimed a sly grin at me, his hand already on the door handle. "I thought I'd let my great-aunt Peg feed us some lunch. You game?"

The scarecrow jerked suddenly toward us in the wind.

"Sure," I responded. "Why not?"

The house had twin chimneys and a gray fieldstone foundation with cellar windows set just above ground level, the hand-blown glass, I noticed, distorting our reflections as we approached. A set of steps led up to a wide front porch with two of Tom's apple-wood rockers positioned at either side of the front door like sentinels. The white paint, layered on the clapboard house again and again for a hundred years, was thick and clean; the place seemed to glow in the cold, pellucid November light.

When we reached the top of the stairs, the front door swung open and Tom's great-aunt, the witch, stepped out on the porch.

"Aunt Peg," he said, stepping forward, "this is my friend, David."

She glanced at me, not speaking, and nodded once. One hand clutched at a black wool shawl that draped over the shoulders of her flowered dress, and a single braid of thick gray hair fell down past the middle of her back. A wicked smile lit her dark eyes as she assessed me. Catching that look, I imagined her hair coal black and the wrinkles gone from her high-boned cheeks, and I understood at once that there was something more basic, more fundamental than magic or spells, that had kept Tom's great-uncle Harry on that farm for all those years.

"Come in out of the wind," she said. "You boys must be hungry."

The voice, coming from that lined face, was surprising: it was a girl's voice, a bird's.

She ushered us inside, down a hallway with a scrap of rag carpet on the hardwood floor. Passing, I glimpsed a parlor to my left—claw-footed chairs, a marble-topped end table, an oak highboy my antique-collecting parents would've killed for—before we emerged in her sunny kitchen. Peg gestured open-handed at the table. There was homemade egg salad, a mason jar of pickles, soup from vegetables out of her garden, wild blackberry cobbler. I'd been living for months on burgers and fries at the Lincoln Diner, and I'd forgotten what real food was like. As we ate, we talked about the harvest, the winter that was coming on, and I enjoyed the brief illusion that I was some prosperous local farmer in a Washington Irving story. Then Tom excused himself to make a phone call, and Peg Henry and I were left measuring each other over the remains of the meal.

"You're from the college, aren't you, David?"

"Yes m'am."

She tipped her head to one side, regarding me with undisguised curiosity. "So what are you doing *here*?"

"Excuse me?"

A simple question, but I was immediately on guard.

"You graduated, didn't you?"

"Yes," I admitted.

"Then why are you still here?" The sun slipped momentarily behind a cloud, and the lines seemed to deepen in a web across her face. "What are you looking for, David? What do you want?"

I took a deep breath, sat back in my chair, and tried to think how to answer her.

"I guess I didn't want this part of my life to end," I offered.

A subtle, negating turn of her head, and the old woman observed me suspiciously from the corners of her eyes. "And what else?"

She wouldn't accept nostalgia as the truth. She wanted the *full* answer, and somehow she'd known exactly what to ask. A cold wave thrilled down my spine.

"Okay," I began, fumbling for words. "There's something here, something in the landscape. Maybe it's in every landscape, I don't know. I've only felt it here. I want to know what it is, but it keeps evading me."

Peg sat regarding me, silent as a cat, her hands folded on the table. I tried again.

"It's like there's another *layer*—do you know what I mean? Something deeper, more profound, but I can't quite get to it." Frustrated, I glared at my empty plate. "It's like seeing something out of the corner of your eye, but when you turn, it's not there."

"And you want a better look. Is that it?"

I glanced up at her. "That's it exactly."

"David," she began, leaning toward me across the table, "do you have any idea what you're doing?"

"Not really," I admitted.

"I thought not. Let me tell you something. Once you've seen something, really seen it, you can never again pretend that you haven't. It changes you. Are you prepared for that?"

For a few seconds our eyes locked, and I felt as if I were looking into a cold, deep well.

"I need to know," I insisted.

She told me then about the orchard, a very old one, at the edge of the foothills northwest of town. Her family owned the land, and the fruit was never harvested. Every winter, the apples hung on the boughs until they dropped.

"Get Tom to show you where it is in the daylight," she suggested. "Two nights from tonight is the new moon. Go out there at midnight, in the dark. Park your car on the orchard road and walk into the trees. When you're out of sight of the road, pick an apple and bite into it."

"What happens then?"

She grinned at me. "You'll see."

AN HOUR LATER, I'd managed to convince myself that Peg Henry was a harmless eccentric who'd lived alone for too long, and I put her story out of my mind. I had no intention of participating in what was, in all likelihood, a practical joke played on a college kid, the local version of a snipe hunt. But that same evening, when Tom and I got back to Musselman's to punch out, I found a pink slip waiting for me. The harvest was in, and they didn't need me anymore. The loss of my job brought a new pressure to bear: my time was running out. I spent the next two days unsuccessfully looking for work; it seemed there was nothing to be found in that town but leaves rustling noisily in the gutters and sunlight growing cold on the brick storefronts. For the first time in my life, I felt the raw wind of the world on my neck. I figured there was one more thing I needed to do before I packed up, defeated, and went home to the future I didn't really want.

So two nights later, some time after eleven o'clock, I found myself wandering the unmarked back roads ten miles or so northwest of town. Not being from the country, I hadn't understood what Peg had meant about the new moon. Far from any streetlights, the night was unimaginably dark. As I rattled along the dirt lanes in my Volkswagen, the headlights, weaving together in the darkness a few feet in front of my windshield, looked like a single match struck in the immensity of a black underground cave. At one point, I was sure I was lost, and what I was doing seemed incredibly silly; but somehow, I managed to find again the road that Tom had showed me. I drove slowly, trying to avoid the potholes that could've easily flattened a tire or bent my axle. After about a hundred yards, I rounded a bend and pulled over, my headlights sweeping the peeling gray and white bark of a huge old sycamore that marked the spot.

Outside the window to my right, the orchard ran downhill into darkness.

When I climbed out of my car, I was momentarily stunned, breathless. The night was flawlessly clear, and the stars, glittering in the darkness overhead, reached from horizon to horizon, touching, even, the black line of hills in the distance. A cold wind trailed past my face, bringing the scent of windfalls.

I paused for a second, uncertain, bemused, observing myself. I had that strange feeling of impending revelation I often sense, even now, on autumn nights. I could smell something coming in the fallen leaves and slowly turning fruit. My anticipation was mixed with a trace of dread I couldn't deny; but having come this far, there was nothing to do but continue. I opened the car door to check my watch by the dome light: it was one minute to twelve. I stepped off downhill into the trees.

Last year's fruit lay cidery and rotten in the tall grass under the unpruned trees, and I was glad I'd worn my work boots. It didn't take long, among that overgrown tangle of branches, to lose sight of my car. Reaching up, I plucked an apple from the nearest tree, rubbed it against the thick wool shirt I wore as a jacket, and bit into it. The apple tasted tarter, wilder somehow, than the fruit I'd been hauling at work. Chewing doggedly, I waited for something to happen, but nothing did. The night was silent, cold, and black around me, and I suddenly felt the absurdity of the circumstance I'd put myself in, standing alone in an orchard in the middle of the night with a sour apple in my hand. I imagined Peg Henry sitting with a hot cup of tea in front of a crackling fire, listening to the sound of the wind rushing outside and laughing her ass off at my expense.

Then I saw it. *The stars*—they were different somehow, closer, as if each star were a planet. And then I realized why they looked so strange: they weren't twinkling. Each star had been frozen in place. The next instant, my mind registered the black forms of the trees around me, neatly shaped now, *pruned*. The smell in the air had changed, as well. None of last year's windfalls were turning in the grass, only the clean trace of ice in the stillness.

My God—it worked! The force of that realization drove me, laughing, to my knees. Was it possible? Somehow, I told myself, I had managed to step out of the world, out of time and process, and the feeling stole suddenly over me that I was being watched. It was as if a spotlight had been turned on me, though there was no break in the absolute blackness of the night. I don't remember how long I lay in the grass, awestruck and ecstatic, staring up at the dark, unmoving sky. But at last, the frozen ground seeped through my jeans and both shirts, chilling me. Shivering, I got to my feet, dropped the apple I'd clutched unknowingly the entire time, and started for my car.

Disoriented, I stepped uphill through the rows of apple trees, the frozen stars seeming to gaze down dispassionately, but my car wasn't where it should've been. After a moment, I found what could've been the sycamore, but there was no road, only a line of barbed wire marking the border of the orchard and a thicket of woods beyond. Something huge was moving in the trees, crashing toward me, coming closer. Quickly, I retraced my steps in the dark. But it was too cold to stay in that orchard all night, and after a few minutes I tried a new direction, still uphill, but at a different angle. No road, no blue Volkswagen waiting to deliver me. Again I retraced my steps. This time I hit a dirt road that seemed familiar, but walking that road repeatedly, I found no sign of my car. It crossed my mind that Tom might've snuck out, hotwired the car, and made off with it; but if that were the case, I would've heard the engine turn over, and the night had been eerily, ponderously silent.

Cold, frustrated, increasingly angry, I crossed and re-crossed that plot of orchard, and finally, just as the light was coming up, I stumbled upon my car—but how I'd failed to do so for so many hours bewildered me. The long grass in the orchard was stiff and white with frost by then. Gratefully, I climbed behind the wheel and started for town.

Three days later, still baffled over my midnight excursion, I reluctantly left those rolling hillsides for suburbia.

MORE THAN THIRTY YEARS have passed since that night of ecstasy and cold confusion. Peg Henry has long since gone back into the fields and hills she loved, and though I asked around when I returned to town one spring for a class reunion, I was never able to get a line on Tom McAdams. I tried to find the orchard road again, but after so many years, I didn't know where to begin to look. After driving around pointlessly for hours, I went back to my hotel, had an extra Scotch, and tried my best to forget about it.

What really happened that night? Nothing maybe, except the

mind playing tricks in the dark. But at the time I didn't think so. So I packed up my strange experience and took it with me, as I did my well-thumbed books and poems, when I finally left that place. To my parents' great relief, I was home by Thanksgiving. They were sure I'd been throwing my life away. I saw no point in trying to argue with them.

I got a job in a hotel in Philadelphia, where the disco music I loathed was pouring by then from all the clubs, and started saving money for my escape. What followed was law school, marriage and children, eventual partnership in my firm, a second house at the beach—all the struggles of life, the getting and spending, and never again a hint of the cool still sky of eternity. Except in my dream. I started having it at law school during exams, and then later when I was trying to pass the bar. Sometimes I still have it, mainly when it's been too long between vacations and the endless, mind-numbing minutia of work seems all there is of life. I'm walking the orchard road in the dark, looking for my car, and I still have that damned apple in my hand. I come upon a house on a rise. A dog on the porch watches me approach: I can see his yellow eyes in the darkness. But, as if he knows me, he doesn't bark, and I go inside. A woman sitting at a table in the glow of a hurricane lamp glances up, startled, when I enter. Her hair is pulled back and parted in the middle, and she's wearing a dark dress with long sleeves, a high neck, full skirts. Her eyes, staring at me, are large and liquid in the flickering light, and there's a terrible urgency on her face. She struggles to speak, but can't. Though I tell myself to wait, to stay and hear the message, I'm unable to remain in the room. I lay what's left of the apple on the table, turn, and hurry away.

Then I wake up. I have no idea what the dream means, but whenever I have it, I go through my day, no matter how hectic, with the calm detachment of a Buddhist monk. For a while at least, nothing really touches me. The people I work with—my associates in the firm, my secretary, long-time clients—have all noticed it. Ever since my night in the orchard, I've lived with one foot in the other world.

Somewhere, I think, in a house on a hill above an apple orchard, a woman sits at a table with a kerosene lamp, an empty chair across from her, a gnawed apple core the only object on the table. For her, I have just left the room. Someday, after I'm dead perhaps, I'll walk back in, and she'll tell me what she was about to say.

The Skinny-dippers

They had started for the island late that afternoon when Glen got home from work and had been driving now for nearly two hours. Their silver BMW rushed smoothly south, having left the snarl of Houston traffic behind, and hardly seemed to touch the road as it glided through the green, smoky summer twilight. The setting sun smeared a band of red across the west, blackening the twisted shapes of live oaks that bordered a pasture. The road was fairly empty, so Glen stepped on the gas, hoping to reach the house they'd rented on South Padre Island while there was still enough light to find their way.

"How much longer, do you think?"

He glanced across at his wife, Carol, as he spoke. She was in the passenger's seat, a road map fanned out haphazardly in her lap. Her coppery brown hair, neatly bobbed at her jaw line, fell forward across her face as she bent to consult the map.

"I don't know. Maybe thirty, forty minutes."

"I hope this place is as nice as the pictures."

Carol shifted in her seat to face him, and the map rustled noisily to her ankles. "Well, if it isn't," she smiled, lifting her chin, "we can always go to Motel 6. It'll be just like it was when we were kids and broke all the time."

Glen smiled ruefully to himself, his eyes fixed on the road, the white lines coming at him out of the twilight in dots and dashes. He'd worked hard for years to get where he was in life, a music retailer with four stores in the greater Houston area, holding his own against the larger chains and the steady encroachment of the Internet. But there had been, inevitably, something lost in the process. He'd opened his first store for the music; it had a force, a wayward vitality he'd wanted to share. Now, all he thought about was business.

"Hey," Carol said, breaking in on his thoughts, "remember that night we went skinny-dipping in the Sandersons' pool?"

Now what made her think of that? he wondered.

But of course he remembered. That was thirty years ago, before they were married. It was 1978, and in a week Glen would leave the Houston suburbs to start college in Austin. He and Carol had spent the summer together, driving to the beach or evading the heat in movie theaters. Then one night in the middle of August, at three in the morning, when the heavy silence in the neighborhood was broken only by the breath of air conditioning systems switching on, Glen had boosted Carol over the wooden privacy fence into the Sandersons' backyard. He'd heard her land safely in the grass and scrambled over the fence after her. By the time he got to his feet, cloaked in the shadow of a massive live oak, he'd spotted Carol Masterson shucking off her bikini bottom as she rushed for the pool, her top already lying behind her on the grass. That had been, he thought, holding the beamer's wheel steady in his hand, the one truly exquisite surprise of his life. Her hair, long and straight then and reaching nearly to the pale swell of her hips, had flowed behind her as she ran. He'd kicked off his cut-offs and followed her, wading after her into water still warm from the day's brutal sun, the clean, sharp bouquet of chlorine filling his head. They'd been careful to bite back their laughter, the ripples their bodies made in the pool sounding much too loud in the stillness as the bedroom windows of the Sanderson place looked down on them like great, lightless eyes.

In some respects, it seemed to Glen Porter that that unexpected interlude, when the risk of discovery and forbidden things had been half the allure, had only just occurred; in other ways, it felt so long ago that it might've happened to entirely different people.

He slid his eyes inquisitively toward his wife and found her watching him.

"You know," she said, running a single manicured nail down his arm, "the place we've rented has a pool."

AN HOUR LATER, Glen sat at the kitchen table in their rented house, the lights dimmed, absently staring out the darkened picture window with an empty beer bottle in front of him. Strange, he had almost forgotten how to relax. Now he felt the beer easing him into a slightly different state of consciousness. Past his ghostly reflection in the glass, he saw the pale slope of the dune topped with ragged sea oats, and beyond it, a glossy black plane he knew was the Gulf of Mexico. Despite the thick plate glass, he could hear the slow, muted crash of wave after wave unfolding on the sand.

Down the hallway to his right, Carol busied herself in the master bedroom, hanging up clothes and arranging tee shirts and underwear in dresser drawers, something she always did to inhabit a new space.

Glen pushed back his chair and stood, stretching with a weary, satisfied groan. He grabbed a second Heineken from the refrigerator and settled back contentedly into his seat. He had to hand it to Carol, she'd found a great place. The two-bedroom stucco house was built on its own sea wall, raising it just above the top of the dune out front, making the place an island unto itself. A deck extended from the front of the house, and stairs led down to the right, where the private pool nestled in the dunes.

A narrow boardwalk snaked from there through the sea oats to the beach, and the fact that there wasn't another house for a hundred yards in either direction added to the sense of isolation.

He realized how hard Carol had worked to find a place where they could be alone. She was the principal of a prestigious middle school in Houston, and the two of them were often too busy, too burdened with the skirmishes of their respective careers, to find adequate time for each other. Thinking of the girl he'd discovered naked in the Sandersons' pool so many years ago, Glen realized, with a stab of regret, that this was a loss he couldn't bear. How had they drifted so far off course? Carol was still beautiful, no question about that. The years appearing in faint lines at the corners of her tawny eyes or in the intermittent strands of gray showing in her copper hair only made her more particular, more interesting, like a coin carrying the nicks and scrapes of its passage through the world.

So here they were. Glen had made it a point not to bring his cell phone. If something went wrong at work, they could damn well figure it out without him for once.

The moon had risen behind the house, high enough now to clear the roof and cast a broad path of light into the Gulf, and Glen's thoughts were interrupted by movement in the water.

Someone, maybe forty yards out, had crawled through the sea across that band of light. As Glen peered through the window, straining to see into the night, a second figure, a woman, swam through the light in the wake of the first.

What the hell are they doing out there? he wondered. Their movements had been graceful and fluid, no sense of a struggle, so they weren't drowning. But something about those white bodies in the dark sea arrested him.

Pushing himself up from the table, he stepped into the living room and through the sliding glass doors to the deck. The low roar of the waves filled the night, and a humid, salt-laden breeze rustled through the sea oats. Leaning forward at the rail, he spotted the swimmers to his right—they stood now waist-deep on the sandbar, moonlight gleaming on the boy's wet shoulders as he embraced his companion. When the girl pushed out of the long-haired boy's arms and started for shore, laughing as she waded awkwardly through the tide, Glen could tell from the easy sway of her breasts that she wasn't wearing a suit.

He heard the door slide open behind him and turned to see Carol step out, wearing a white terrycloth robe and rubbing her hair dry with a towel as the wind blew it back.

"What's up?" she asked, sidling up behind him.

"Nothing much," he smiled. "A couple of kids out there are having a little naked swim."

"Really? Where?"

When he glanced back at the beach, intending to point out their faintly luminescent shapes in the darkness, they were nowhere to be seen.

LATER THAT NIGHT, already under the spell of the place, Glen Porter crawled into bed next to his wife, closed his eyes, and drifted easily into sleep . . .

He was standing on the beach in the darkness, the rush of the waves in his ears. A fog had rolled in off the sea, erasing the bungalows in the distance, and as he turned, trying to get his bearings, he heard a woman crying out. The sound arrived vaguely, muffled by fog and the steady exhalation of the waves.

The voice was calling him, repeating his name.

Searching, he stepped tentatively forward, feeling the sand cool and damp under his bare feet. Fog closed around him like spun cotton, and then, in the distance, he spotted something—a dark shape twisting, struggling on the sand. The voice, he realized, was coming from that undefined shape, and as he approached, he knew what he was seeing.

The boy lay on top of his lover, holding himself up by his locked arms, her legs wrapped around the small of his back. She cried out as he thrust repeatedly into her.

They were still for a moment, feeling Glen's eyes on them, then turned their heads to him in unison. Untangling themselves, they scrambled to their knees and stood, a pair of linked silhouettes, the boy reaching protectively for the girl's hand. They were shapes without features, cut-outs from the night sky—full of starlight, Glen thought, if only he could touch them. But when he stepped forward, his hand reaching out, they turned and ran.

He started after them, saw them break out of the fog before him, their pale legs scissoring in the moonlight as they flew over the sand. Trapped in the urgency of dream, Glen sprinted after them, forcing himself to move faster, his heart pounding, lungs burning for air. They ran shoulder to shoulder, beautiful, he thought, in the first full possession of their prime. The girl's long hair, reaching past her waist, flew behind her as she ran, and Glen came closer, closer, until his fingers tangled in her hair and she cried out . . .

When he woke, sunlight angled into the room through the blinds. He heard a gull call, and the shadow of wings moved over the shuttered window.

"DID YOU HEAR our visitors last night?"

Carol placed a mug of coffee in front of him on the kitchen table as she spoke. She slid into an adjacent chair and tipped her oval face into one hand to observe him.

"I didn't hear much of anything," Glen replied, not really awake yet. "I slept like a rock." Then, realizing what she'd said, he asked, "What visitors?"

"A couple, I assume. They were using the pool. I didn't see

them very well, but I *heard* her," Carol grinned. "She was making a fair amount of noise, the little vixen. I'm surprised they didn't wake you."

Glen's dream came back to him in pieces: the crying out in the fog; the dark shape, formless at first, on the sand. A vague uneasiness tugged at him.

"I don't like the idea of strangers hanging around this place at night," he said.

Carol shrugged. "Just two kids, trying to find a place to be alone. You remember what that was like, don't you?"

"Yeah, I guess."

"They probably didn't realize there was anyone here. Tonight," she suggested, "we'll leave a light on in the living room. That should discourage them."

As Carol showered and dressed, Glen took his coffee out on the deck, squinting against the bright morning light knifing off the surface of the Gulf. It promised to be a flawless day, and he made an effort to push away the last of the night's cobwebs and shadows. Downing his coffee, Glen left the empty mug by the sliding glass doors and wandered absent-mindedly down the steps to the pool. The clear water sparkled, emitting diamonds of light, and his eyes took in the fifty-foot expanse with a proprietary satisfaction. Then he spotted something in the shallow end at his feet. He waded in to retrieve the object floating there like a jellyfish.

As he'd thought: it was a bikini top. He climbed out of the pool and examined it. Dirty white and orange stripes, thoroughly sun-faded, the straps frayed. There was a brown smear of tar, he noted, on one of the cups.

She must've loved the thing: she'd worn it to death.

Glen walked his find up to the house and laid it on the kitchen counter. Turning away, intending to change into drier clothes, he met Carol, combed and sweet-smelling, just stepping into the kitchen, her short white skirt and sleeveless top showing off her tan. She carried a straw purse with palm trees slung over one shoulder, ready to go.

"Take me to breakfast?" she suggested. Then, noticing his shorts, she asked, "How'd you get wet?"

"Pulling *that* out of the pool," Glen told her, gesturing behind him to the counter.

Carol's eyes slid curiously to the top. She moved toward it, paused, then stepped forward and snatched it up. Glen watched her back, her head bent over the faded cloth.

"Apparently," he commented, "she didn't bother to get dressed when she left."

Carol turned to him, her eyes heavy with a question, but said nothing. Then, decided, she walked the top to the glossy metal trashcan in the corner and shoved it in. Putting on a tight smile, she said, "C'mon, take me to breakfast. I'm starving."

GLEN PORTER STRETCHED OUT on a lounger on the sand. He let the July sun carry his mind away until there was only light flashing on water, the sound of waves, the occasional plaintive call of a gull. He soon drifted into a state between sleep and waking. Once, he was certain that some uninvited stranger stood silently over him, insistent, casting a thin shadow. But when Glen opened his eyes there was no one there.

He and Carol took a walk on the beach, sorting through the bright clutter of shells cast up at the tide line: pieces of lightning whelk, cockle shells, pink or fuchsia cochinas still attached in pairs like miniscule butterfly wings. Glen wasn't sure how far they'd gone before they turned around—time and distance seemed impossible to judge—but when they got within sight of their setup, he pulled up short.

"Someone's in our place," he said, his voice flat with disbelief.

"What?"

Carol looked up from the shells at her feet and shaded her eyes, looking where Glen pointed. A furrow appeared between her eyes.

The chairs were easy to spot: they occupied the center of a wide circle of empty sand, no one else near. But both chairs were in use. Even at a distance, Glen could make out a pair of intruders, dark against the glare of the sand, reclining in the loungers where they didn't belong. Instinctively, he felt for the house key in the pocket of his swim trunks.

Glen told himself that it was innocent, that they'd been worn out from the heat and simply needed to sit and rest. But gazing at the way the couple had claimed their chairs—not sitting but lying back with their arms behind their heads with a sense of ownership—he knew that wasn't so. The sun beat down, and his head swam with anger.

He hurried forward, intending to confront them, but before he and Carol had closed half the distance between themselves and the intruders, the pair sat up suddenly, in unison, and turned toward them. The next instant they were up, out of the chairs, looking in the distance like two stick figures drawn by a child, their indistinct forms wavering in the heat rising from the sand. Glen heard laughter as they ran off down the beach, holding hands, and lost themselves in the cluster of sun-worshippers in the distance.

A swim in the sea helped restore his calm, and an hour later, he and Carol folded up their loungers and headed for the boardwalk that led past the pool to the house. Seeing her struggle with the chair, Glen took it from her and followed behind as Carol made her way through the dunes and shoulder-high sea oats. When he arrived at the pool, he found her standing absolutely still, staring into the water, her back straight as a flagpole.

"What is it?" he asked. "What's wrong?"

Dropping the loungers, he followed the line of her gaze. The bikini top floated close to the edge where they stood, and Glen kneeled to retrieve it.

He got to his feet, exasperated, the wet rag dripping in his hand. It seemed a deliberate message, a threat or an insult scrawled like a note across the bright afternoon. Carol grabbed the top from his hand, examining the frayed straps, the single tar stain, tear-shaped, on one of the orange-striped cups.

"Glen," she informed him with a nervous laugh, "this is the *same* top. It's identical."

"I thought you threw that thing away."

Her eyes, wide behind the lenses of her sunglasses, met his. "I did."

Without a word, Glen turned and started for the house. Using his key, he entered through the sliding glass doors and quickly checked the living room—nothing out of place. Stepping into the kitchen, he searched the trash and found the bikini top missing. Then he headed down the hall to the master bedroom.

He paused in the doorway, suddenly dizzy; then gathered himself and edged toward the bed with labored slowness, deliberately, as if he were wading through water. Glen came to himself standing with his knees against the edge of the mattress, staring down at the bed in frustrated disbelief. The skin on the back of his neck and sun-burned shoulders contracted in a cold wave.

The comforter and top sheet had been pulled back and kicked partway to the floor. The bottom sheet kept the clear impression of two bodies, the pillows dented by a pair of heads. Glen bent to lay a palm on the mattress: the sheet was still damp. He saw the two of them stealing up from the pool, entering the house, lying face to face in a stranger's bed, touching, the chance of discovery giving the interlude its urgency, its compelling sense of risk . . .

On one of the pillows, Glen found a long, sun-bleached brown hair.

Something moved in the corner of his eye, and he swung around to find Carol leaning in the doorway, watching him. He hadn't heard her approach.

Her eyes went to the bed and then sought his. There was no need to explain; she understood at once what had happened.

A QUICK INVENTORY of their belongings showed that nothing was missing. Glen was relieved to discover that, but in a way, it left him even more unsettled. Robbery, at least, was a motive he could understand.

Checking the doors and windows, he found no sign of a break-in, so he had to assume the intruders had a key. As Carol changed the sheets in the master bedroom, he lost no time in contacting the realtor and telling her what had happened, and that same evening, before the light was gone, they had new locks on all the doors and a brand new set of keys.

Worn out from the sun and his own perplexity, Glen fell immediately to sleep that night. He dreamed he was on the beach, seeing those kids rising from the loungers in the distance, their shapes wavering in the heat. He called out to them, taking after them when they ran—the boy with his long dark hair and broad shoulders, the girl with her waist-length hair like a mermaid—and as he closed the distance between them, they stepped into the air like birds. Smothered laughter turned into the cry of gulls, and they were gone . . .

He woke with a start, instantly alert, staring intently at the ceiling. Carol slept peacefully beside him, an arm thrown over his chest, but he knew he'd heard something: a noise in the house had yanked him violently from sleep. A house, any house, makes sounds in the dark; but as Glen slowed his breath and concentrated to listen, he heard something else, something beyond the expected pops and creaks and the steady breath of waves in the distance. He knew at once what it was. Someone had placed a glass on the polished granite counter in the kitchen.

Spilling silently out of bed, Glen slipped on a robe and crept down the hall. The kitchen was empty—but his pulse leapt when he saw the glass standing by the sink. Grasping the wooden handle of the carving knife, he drew it slowly from the rack on the counter, careful not to make a sound, and stepped into the living room: the silk-covered couch in shadow, the coffee table, the blind gray eye of the television. He was startled for an instant by his own reflection staring back at him, knife in hand, from the sliding glass doors.

Then he heard, faintly, a step in the second bedroom.

He crossed the living room in a few strides and glided stealthily down the hall. The bedroom door stood open. Tightening his grip on the knife, Glen took a moment to peer into the dark. He thought he heard, barely discernible, the sound of someone breathing.

Steeling himself, he stepped into the room.

As his eyes adjusted, he made out the twin beds, the night table between them, the windows with their blinds drawn. Holding his breath, Glen swung open the closet door—empty, not so much as a box or a hanger. Yet someone listened intently as he did, trying not to stir. Glen moved slowly, tensely, toward the far bed, expecting at any instant to confront the intruder, but no one crouched behind it. He dropped to his knees, intending to look *under* the bed, when he caught a glimpse of motion over his shoulder.

He swung around in time to see the boy slide like a shadow out of the room. Scrambling to his feet, Glen heard footsteps retreating, heard the glass doors slide open and closed again before he'd made it out of the bedroom and halfway down the hall. Stumbling into the living room, he discovered Carol standing wide-eyed in the kitchen doorway, holding the robe closed at her throat as she gazed after the intruder.

"He went out there," she said, pointing to the back deck, an odd smile on her face. Spotting the knife in his fist, she added, "Don't hurt him!"

Glen caught sight of the back of the boy's head through the glass, his dark hair spilling over his shoulders as he moved nimbly down the steps. By the time Glen made it to the top of those steps, the boy was already at the far edge of the pool. It was a black night, clouds off the Gulf obscuring the moon, but he could see the boy kneeling at the water, a hand extended to help the girl up, saw the water shining darkly on her hip as she rose from the pool.

They sprinted together for the boardwalk that led to the beach, and in an instant, the pair had vanished in the darkness.

LATE THE FOLLOWING AFTERNOON, Glen leaned back in his rusting lounger on the sand, his fingers linked behind his neck as he gazed out to sea. He watched, distractedly, an undulating line of pelicans that sailed over the breakers parallel to shore. Last night, after the intruders had disappeared, Glen had gone immediately to the kitchen and picked up the phone.

"What're you doing?" Carol had wanted to know. She was leaning in the doorway, that same crooked smile on her face.

"What the hell do you think I'm doing? I'm calling the police." His bewilderment, finding no relief, had morphed into angry frustration.

She approached and laid a slim palm on his sleeve. "Don't," was all she said.

But the idea of doing nothing, of letting this shadow game go on unchecked, was impossible for him to grasp. When he hesitated, the dial tone droning in his hand, she gently took the phone from him and laid it in its charger.

"We can't just let these two run loose in our lives," Glen insisted. And when she didn't respond, he asked, "Aren't you afraid?"

He saw the thought turning in her eyes before she answered. "Yes, in a way I *am* afraid. Maybe that's not the right word. *Awed*, perhaps. But I'm not worried about my safety. Or yours."

With that, she kissed him on the cheek and turned for the bedroom.

Unable to sleep, Glen had sat up in the living room with a lamp on, keeping watch, trying to figure out what Carol had meant; and now, hours later, he was still no closer to understanding her strange lack of concern. Squinting in the glare, Glen Porter glanced across at the woman stretched out in the lounge chair next to his, his wife for over twenty-five years, his lover for longer than that. She lay in the sun with a knowing, Sphinx-like smile on her face, in possession of a secret she wasn't sharing.

Carol felt his glance and opened one eye. "Still worried?"

"I want to know what's going on," he admitted. "Doesn't this bother you? I mean, for all we know, they could be up at the house right now, going through our things, using our bed for Chrissake!"

She shifted in her chair to face him, one leg draping over the other, her head propped in her hand. "Well," she drawled, looking at him over the tops of her sunglasses, "if we went up and used the bed ourselves, then they wouldn't be able to, would they?"

Her tawny eyes seemed heavy in the heat, and a breeze ruffled her short, coppery hair, moving a few fine strands over one cheek. Charmed, somewhat, out of his funk, Glen smiled back at her.

WHEN HE WOKE it was dark. The place next to him in bed was vacant, the covers thrown back. Stealing a look at the clock,

Glen was surprised to discover that it was nearly midnight, and looking farther, he saw his wife through the open bathroom door. She was standing naked in the Jacuzzi, parting the blinds with two fingers to peak out at the pool.

"What're you up to in there?" he asked. But he had a sick feeling he already knew.

Carol stepped out of the tub and approached. Snatching her robe from a chair as she passed, she slipped it on and sat on the edge of the bed, hooking her hair behind one ear.

"Get up, sleepyhead," she said. "I want to show you something."

"What is it?"

She smiled and shook her head. "You wouldn't believe me if I told you. You have to see this for yourself." Patting his leg, she stood. "C'mon," she coaxed. "Come with me."

Glen found his robe and followed her down the hall, and the two of them emerged on the deck. There was a full moon and no clouds, so the night had a silvery, dream-like quality, stars scattered over them, the waves sounding closer in the clear air. Carol grabbed his hand and led him down to the pool, stepping aside at the bottom of the stairs so he could see.

The girl's form wavered palely in the water, her hair spread out behind her like seaweed.

At the far end of the pool, the boy stood without a stitch, turned away, water dripping from his bare legs and torso. Feeling himself observed, he turned, and for the first time, Glen got a good look at his face. A current of shock coursed down his spine, freezing him to the spot.

Glen Porter stood staring at himself at age eighteen, wasp-waisted, his long black hair without a touch of gray spilling to his shoulders. Sheepishly, the boy grinned and raised a hand in greeting.

Seeing this gesture, the girl at his feet swung around in the water, and Glen found himself staring at the face he remembered from that long-ago summer. She paddled to the ladder and climbed out of the pool, light gleaming on her wet skin, the water running in streams from her waist-length hair. Shyly, she stepped to the boy's side and took his hand.

Across the lucid, moonlit expanse of the pool, the two couples, eighteen and nearly fifty, stood regarding each other. A minute, maybe two, passed in complete silence; then, without a word, the midnight intruders turned and glided down the boardwalk through the dunes. In the stillness, Glen heard the sound of bare feet on boards, and in a moment they were gone, swallowed up in the milky dark.

For the rest of their time in that house, Glen and Carol Porter spent their days on the beach, sunning and walking, swimming in the sea; and at night, as they lay face to face in the king bed, touching, their ghosts circled the house and slipped into the pool. Glen would hear, faintly in the darkness, the sound of ripples and laughter—then silence, only the surf, and the immense, unspoken suggestion that the pool was ready for them.

They never bothered to dress when they went down together. Glen followed her, as he had so many years before, and held his breath, watching as she slipped like silk into the water.

Covered Bridge Road

The bridge was made of pine, rough-hewn and stained to look like redwood, a shoebox with a peaked roof built when the first houses in the subdivision were being framed. A winding road, the main route through the neighborhood, passed through the shadowy interior where pigeons roosted in the cross-beams, their wings clapping when a passing car scared them up. The bridge spanned a muddy, chemical-smelling creek, and on one side, the last bit of woods not bull-dozed for houses ran along the stream all the way to the next township.

Thinking back as his plane descended, Duncan was surprised to discover the hold that scene exerted on his imagination. The bridge, after all, was only a piece of deliberately constructed nostalgia, new but made to seem old; it was smoke and mirrors, something to make the harried suburbanites occupying their salt-box or Dutch colonial houses feel connected to the past, like the American eagles they centered above their two-car garages. But Duncan knew that if he'd gotten down his sketchpad from the overhead bin, he could've easily drawn the place, captured it down to the smallest detail. He saw the bridge from below, as if he were looking up at the road from the edge of the woods.

Duncan Roberts was an art historian, an academic on sabbatical. He was working on an article on Cézanne, one that he hoped would secure his promotion and his future. He planned to spend time at the city art museum and at the Barnes Foundation (both had important Cézannes he needed to see), then drive to New York to take in the transcendent still lifes at the Met: apples spilling from blue bowls across a wooden table. He had a cousin living on the Main Line whom he hadn't seen in years, and he hoped, if time allowed, to get in touch for a reunion. But when his plane passed the Philadelphia skyline going east and banked southwest to turn back for the airport, Duncan found himself diverted, unexpectedly looking down at a map of his past.

How had he managed, for over twenty years, to give so little thought to that place? There was something there for him, he was suddenly sure of it—something under the grown-in expanse of trees he looked down on from the window of his jammed commuter flight.

And so, at four-fifteen on a warm afternoon in mid-April, the light just beginning to decline, Duncan Roberts turned off the highway into the neighborhood where he'd grown up. He drove slowly, following the meandering curves of Covered Bridge Road, past the same four house models repeated again and again. The street names—Greenmeadow Lane, Ashgrove Drive—seemed less pretentious now that the trees had grown in, hiding the telephone wires and spreading thick blue shade over the lawns.

Two teenage boys were playing catch in the street. As he passed, Duncan heard the ball strike the one boy's glove with a crisp *smack*!

He parked in the shadow of the bridge. The peaked roof cast a knifepoint over the hood of his rented Taurus, and he walked out over the muddy stream. Leaning at the rail, Duncan gazed down at his reflection in the slow-moving water. He found it strange beyond words to be standing there. Twenty yards of meadow ran along the far side of the creek, and then the tangle of saplings and the larger oaks and maples rising above them in a thick canopy, newly green in the first full flush of spring.

Everything was precisely the same. He felt as if the scene before him, familiar down to the slightest particulars, had waited unchanged all these years for his return. The trees shook and flowed in the breeze, and the freshness of the woods mingled with the stale smell of the stream. Without consciously meaning to, Duncan had banished from his life the time he'd spent here. The events preceding his escape to college felt as if they'd happened to someone else, to a character in a book he barely remembered. But now he sensed the past crowding back, nuzzling his hand like a dog that wanted to be fed. He recalled how he'd used these woods for privacy, for secrecy, and the names and faces of two or three girls he thought he'd forgotten glided across his mind with startling clarity.

There was a girl he'd like who lived at the top of the hill. One evening in July, her father had caught them coming out of the woods together at twilight. Her father, an ex-marine, had gone looking for his daughter when she didn't come home for dinner. Duncan remembered the steely look the man had trained on him from behind the wheel of his idling Oldsmobile.

An unexpected silence imprinted itself on Duncan's awareness, drawing him suddenly out of reverie. Not a single blackbird whistled from the trees, and in the eaves behind him, the rustling, cooing pigeons had gone still, as if they were holding their breath to listen. The sun dropped behind a cloud, draining the world of color, and Duncan was abruptly certain he was being watched.

Unsettled, he scanned the trees. *There*, at the border of the woods, across the meadow punctuated by daisies and bright yellow dandelions, stood a figure washed in patches of light and shadow. Duncan squinted, unsure at first, but *yes*—it was a boy, maybe seventeen, in torn jeans and a tee shirt, barefoot, his straight brown hair reaching past his shoulders. The breeze picked up, and the flowing shade made the boy seem insubstantial, as if he were being continually erased. But Duncan could feel the eyes fixed on him, staring—the gaze intrusive, demanding. What on earth did he want? A sudden gust lifted the branches, immersing the boy briefly in sunlight, and then he was gone.

He never saw the boy leave. But in the sudden light he'd glimpsed his face, roped with scars even at a distance, *burned*. Duncan stepped quickly toward his car.

HE DIDN'T DRIVE BACK to the city. Instead, Duncan booked a room at the Sheraton on the highway and went immediately to the bar, leaving his bags in the trunk of the Taurus. What he'd seen was impossible, and two double shots of bourbon on the rocks did nothing to help him invent an explanation. An hour later, in his room, he threw himself down on the bed and flicked on the television. But he soon muted the sound and lay back on the musty blue spread, listening to the distant rush of traffic.

Duncan had first met Michael Willet in their sophomore English class. His growing friendship with the boy gave Duncan his first glimpse of a world beyond the ordered streets of his suburban neighborhood. The books Willet urged on him—*Steppenwolf*, *The Doors of Perception*, Rimbaud's *Illuminations*—were far more interesting than the required reading for class, and the two of them began to talk about powders that could clear and deepen perception, drugs that would open doors in the mind and cause the veil to fall away from the temporal world.

Remembering, Duncan couldn't suppress an embarrassed smile. If wisdom were so easily acquired, then every crack-head on the street would be a visionary. But lying on the bed in his sterile hotel room, he felt a newly awakened longing for a time in his life when immense possibilities seemed nearly within reach.

One afternoon, he'd gone home with Willet, riding the yellow school bus to a neighborhood he'd never seen before. The houses were older, smaller, the trees lush and dense, shading doorways and gables as they wouldn't do for years yet on Duncan's newer and more affluent street. Willet's mother hung over them, too solicitous, a little hysterical, a woman in turquoise stretch pants and a nylon sweater; and when at last they broke away, his new friend took Duncan wordlessly into the garage and showed him where his father kept a hidden bottle of Jim Beam. They both took a healthy swig—it burned like nothing Duncan had tasted before—and then Willet topped the bottle at an outside spigot and tucked it back behind the cluster of rakes, shovels, and trimming shears. They stretched out in the grass beneath a huge maple in the backyard, letting the bourbon lick through their skulls as they watched the light dance in the breezy depths of the tree.

He was still there when Willet's father got home. In his rumpled khaki suit, he reminded Duncan of ashes. He could smell death on the man, and with a sudden flash of intuition, he understood why his friend's mother was so tense and desperate.

That spring, the two boys were loitering one morning in a back stairwell at school, avoiding the cattle-call of homeroom for as long as possible. He could still see the tile at their feet, its dripped pattern like a bad Jackson Pollock. Willett was imitating their science teacher, Mr. Reiggert, the way he talked through his nose and grunted with satisfaction whenever a Bunsen burner snapped into flame.

"Remember the day he leaned too close and singed off his eyebrows?" Duncan asked.

Willet started laughing. Once he started, he could never stop. His face turned bright red as he struggled for breath, his hair spilling forward, and he collapsed, falling back against a set of doors they assumed were locked. But the doors banged open, revealing an expanse of morning light—fifty yards of school grounds, then a field so green it burned their eyes, a stand of apple trees flowering on a rise beyond the field. Their eyes met for an instant, and then they were sprinting across the grounds and uphill through the calf-deep alfalfa, thumb-sized grasshoppers spitting and whirling away from them as they forced their legs up the slope. At the crest of the rise, closer and closer, loomed the cluster of blooming trees, the white flowers so dense and bright as they approached that it seemed as if some cold fragment of paradise had broken loose and drifted down to settle on that ridge. The boys collapsed under the trees, panting, the May sunlight piercing the translucent blooms.

When they finally caught their breath, Willet dug into the pocket of his jeans, extracting a square of foil and unfolding it gingerly.

"What's that?" Duncan asked.

His friend grinned at him.

"What is it?" he repeated, crawling through the grass for a better look. A scattering of honeybees droned in the air above them.

"Windowpane."

Against the crinkled foil, he saw what looked like two tiny chips of green glass. When Duncan directed an uncomprehending glance at his friend, Willet added, "You know, acid."

The two boys smiled at each other nervously. Over their heads, the white flowers lifted in a breeze.

What he could remember of the rest of that otherworldly day drifted across his mind in pieces: trucks rumbling past on the highway, a heat mirage melting the world at the vanishing point. They'd decided to hitchhike to the sea, and four college girls had picked them up in a white convertible. A girl with long red hair, beautiful hair that fell past her waist, had perched in Duncan's lap like a mermaid, the sun gleaming on her teeth as the wind rushed past. When they'd arrived at Asbury Park, the sea had been wild and jagged, a heaving expanse of cut glass and foam. Somehow, they found their way back. By dusk, they'd been drawn instinctively to the bridge, and they wandered the stretch of woods until the effects of the drug wore off. When he arrived home, hours late, his parents were furious. They were standing by the door when he entered, his father's arms folded across his chest, his mother's gray eyes bright with anger. Behind them, he saw the darkened living room, the shape of the sectional couch, the round oak coffee table, the black mouth of the fireplace. Twice a year, when guests came, the room was put to use. The rest of the time it sat silent and empty, a sign of all the mute subtexts of that house. He couldn't recall what he told them.

Rousing himself, Duncan glanced at the bedside clock. He was surprised to see that it was half past eight, the night pushing its black muzzle up against the window. He switched on a lamp and went downstairs to get something to eat before the dining room closed.

THE NEXT MORNING, Duncan made it a point to get an early start. By nine-fifteen, he had crossed back to the city and was walking up the front steps toward the massive Corinthian pillars of the Philadelphia Museum of Art. Under his arm, he carried a notebook large enough to include sketches, if necessary, as well as his written notes.

Duncan was fascinated by Cézanne's career. Though he painted from the time he was a young man, Cézanne never did anything truly his own until he was nearly forty, and most of his finest work was done within a few years of his death. Duncan needed to understand an obsession that could last through so many years of near misses and partial success. His intention was to trace Cézanne's evolution from the early, basically mimetic work to the late masterpieces, where the painter was transforming landscape into its underlying geometric patterns. He wanted to follow this progression through a handful of particular paintings, work he hadn't specifically chosen yet, and the museum's collection, which housed canvases from the 1870s up to the painter's death in 1906, was a fertile place to begin fleshing out his ideas. The editor of *ARTnews*, an old acquaintance from graduate school, had indicated that he would welcome such a piece, and Duncan knew that an article featured in a prestigious journal, beautifully illustrated, would virtually assure his promotion and tenure.

So he paid his entrance fee, turned eagerly from the counter, and stepped into the air-conditioned and humidity-controlled interior of the museum. Without hesitation, he swung right, into the interlocking maze of the Annenberg Galleries.

He knew exactly where to go. A group of uniformed schoolchildren on a class trip were ushered out of the room as he entered, whispering in asides; they were fifth-graders, he guessed, the same age as his daughter.

Left to himself, Duncan felt the silence form solidly around him. The high ceilings, the light falling from above, and the soft tile floors designed to deaden sound made him feel as if he'd entered a chapel just emptied of its congregation. The Monets and Pissarros, the lush Renoirs—everything was familiar, and the sense of return crashed down on him again. He hadn't walked through these rooms or stood before these actual canvases in years, and he realized, with a shock, that the last time he'd been here was with Michael Willet. They'd cut school and gone to the museum together. How had he forgotten that?

Doggedly, he sat on a bench in front of *Mont Sainte-Victoire* and opened his notebook.

He trained his eye on the canvas, the yellow blocks of buildings and dark green cypresses rising to the massive blue crown of the mountain. But the houses and trees recalled yesterday's light and shadow and the figure he believed he'd seen there, and his concentration strayed.

The strange awakening he'd undergone as a boy with Michael

Willet had been vital but terrifying, and perhaps that was why, when he'd finally broken loose from all that self-immolating wonder and confusion, he had refused for so many years to give those events a place in his life. Each new step he'd taken with his friend had been a release and a violation, and with each new adventure, it became more and more difficult to come back to any sort of ordered reality. Remembering, Duncan realized that Willet had never intended to come back. After their bent, visionary journey to the sea, his friend lost interest in forbidden books and talk. Only direct experience would do, and he took it as a maxim never to repeat himself, always to go farther. Duncan found himself less and less willing to follow his friend blindly on these excursions, and a rift began to open between them.

By the time they graduated, Willet was in some altered state of consciousness all the time, and the two of them hardly spoke anymore. One night in August, shortly after midnight, Duncan had come across his friend unexpectedly at the bridge. Willet perched on the railing, feet dangling loosely over the stream, his attention fixed on the silver half moon suspended above the black shape of the trees. He had an old bandana tied around his head, with a red chrysanthemum, plucked from someone's flower bed, tucked in back.

"What's up, chief?" Duncan had asked.

"Me," came the hollow reply.

For a moment, Duncan couldn't think of a thing to say, but he needed to say something.

A spark had blown out in his life.

"Remember that day we cut school and went to Philly?" he offered at last. "We walked all the way to Haddonfield to catch the train. Then spent the day in Fairmount Park and the museum."

Willet tipped his head quizzically. His eyes narrowed in concentration, as if he were translating from a language imperfectly understood. His response, when it came, traveled across a chasm, a voice in a dream.

"I remember." Then, "Doing any painting?" he asked.

"No," Duncan shrugged. "Not really."

"*No*, of course not."

The phrase arrived with a weight of derision, carrying all the bitterness of their old disagreement. Duncan was stung into silence. Then Willet broke out in high-pitched laughter, the laughter that, once started, never seemed to stop. It cut Duncan as he walked away, leaving the dark, moon-silvered box of the covered bridge behind him.

Two weeks later, Willet turned over the camper he was driving on a back road and was trapped in the cab when the engine caught fire. A witness to the accident pulled him out, but Willet was burned over half his body, including his face, and blood tests indicated that he'd had enough barbiturates in his system to tranquilize an elephant. Duncan went to see him in the hospital. They had him in a plastic isolation tent—with so much raw flesh exposed, the risk of infection was alarming. Duncan gazed through the translucent plastic at that ruined face, and it was like seeing it under water or through the wavering lens of a dream. Suddenly the eyes opened and met his, staring, brimming over with pain and cold accusation.

Duncan met that glare for as long as he could, then turned and left the room.

Three days after that, Michael Willet was dead. On the day of the funeral, Duncan was three hundred miles away on a red-brick campus in the foothills of the Allegany Mountains, beginning his new life. He never looked back.

Until now.

The air-conditioning switched on with a soft, nearly inaudible breath. Duncan watched the slow parade of visitors trailing contemplatively along the rows of canvases, necks craned forward, their arms behind their backs. Leaving his empty notebook on the bench, he stepped through the adjoining gallery, pushed through the men's room door, and found himself alone in a cool, white-tile room. Bending over the sink, he splashed some water in his face and looked up to search his eyes in the mirror.

What was I supposed to do, he asked himself, *follow him into the fire?*

But that was exactly what he *had* done, and then turned away as his friend plunged blindly ahead. He had saved his own life, but at a cost. Willet had shown him something, had opened a door Duncan hadn't known was there. Having caught a glimpse, he'd hung around on the outskirts of mystery all his life, but always at one remove. He'd gotten the degrees, published a few articles; and indeed, there was nothing wrong with being a critic. But he wasn't a critic. He was a painter who didn't paint.

His whole life! The sink swam before his eyes, a frozen white lily, and he grasped it with both hands to steady himself.

IT WAS ALMOST DARK when Duncan swung onto Covered Bridge Road, his pale headlights probing the April shadows. Twilight was busy erasing the boundaries of sky and trees, blurring everything into a single darkness. At the bottom of a rise, a road spun off to the left, and he remembered that Michael Willet had lived down there. He turned and soon found himself driving past the shapes of old houses in the dark. Here and there, a yellow window spilled its light onto a dark lawn. Hanging ferns were silhouetted on railed front porches; on one of them a swing, suspended from a length of chain, creaked slightly in the breeze.

But there was no trace of his old friend here, not on this newly gentrified lane. Turning around in a driveway, hc found his way back to the main road.

As he entered the streets of his own neighborhood, the one he'd grown up in, Duncan recited to himself the names of families who'd lived in the houses he passed, kids he'd gone to school with twenty or thirty years before. He crested a hill, and his headlights aimed down suddenly at a bend in the road, at a peaked shape rising like an iceberg in the dark. The black bridge loomed into view, and Duncan, obeying an impulse, pulled to the side, scanning the impenetrable wall of trees to his left.

Nothing moved. After a moment, he put the engine in park and rolled down his window. The sound of crickets filled up the car like water, drowning out the low drone of the idling motor. He sensed someone waiting in the trees, just out of sight, as if this unseen figure had stepped back at a threshold, daring him to enter.

Throwing open the door, Duncan Roberts stepped out of the car, slipped down the embankment, and strode through the tall weeds and wildflowers to the edge of the woods. He listened intently, silently, cold at the bone. Wind lifted the dark branches. To his right, he heard the stream slide past and caught its dank, stale odor. He was certain that someone watched as he did, breathing faintly, straining to hear, close enough to smell the weeds his steps had crushed.

"Okay!" he shouted into the shifting, rustling trees. "I'm here now. What do you want from me?"

As he stood there, waiting, the dew soaking his shoes, a picture rose up in his mind. A boy raced ahead uphill through a green field wavering and burning in the wind, his sense of release tangible in the gold morning light. The boy was running from his dying father, from his brittle mother, running out of the world toward a stand of white trees flowering in the distance . . .

When Duncan turned at last to climb back to his idling car, the door left open and the dome light glowing in the dark, a shadow detached itself from the trees to go with him, moving as he did, so close he could feel the dead boy's breath on his neck. Clambering up the slick embankment, Duncan slid behind the wheel and pulled the door closed. He glanced nervously into the rearview mirror, expecting to be confronted by a pair of eyes in a burned, ravaged face.

But just then a car topped the rise behind him. Its high-beams flared in the mirror, blinding him, and he put the Taurus in gear and drove on.

The Emissary

One evening at the end of June, as David Wilkins wandered through the produce section of his neighborhood grocery store after work, he glanced across a table piled high with yellow apples and saw a man step past, bent over slightly and mumbling incoherently to himself, an empty basket hooked over his emaciated arm. At that moment, David realized he'd seen the man before—though he couldn't recall when or where—and then, unaccountably, he began seeing him nearly everywhere he went. Stepping past the colorful cartoon mural in the parking lot of his favorite coffee shop, he'd enter to find the old man slumped at a back table, nursing a cup of the house blend and staring out pensively at the clientele with his washed-out blue eyes. At the book store, when David headed for the register with an armful of paperbacks, he'd spot the man in the mystery section, back turned, the white hair sticking up rakishly at the back of his skull as he contemplated the spines of the latest thrillers.

At first, David thought this was nothing more than coincidence, some unexpected confluence of events that placed the stranger repeatedly in his path. Baffled but unconcerned, he shrugged, went on with his life, and did his best to put these episodes out of his mind.

David Wilkins painted angels. His job at the museum gave

him enough, barely, to pay the rent on an old brick house in the Montrose district, a place with room for a studio where he lived alone. No one passing him on the street, his six-foot frame crowned with curly black hair and quick green eyes, would've guessed that he spent so much time knocking at the door of another world. But David was obsessed. He struggled to give expression to the life he felt lurking behind this one. Calling out repeatedly, he waited for an answer that never seemed to arrive. So he painted, and he frequented his favorite cafés and restaurants, waiting for the moment when the traffic and trees would drift away like smoke to reveal the place his mind imagined.

One afternoon in July, David stood at his easel in the back bedroom, sunlight pouring in, stalled in his effort to find what he wanted in the painting before him. At such times, his hope grew as thin and brittle as his patience. Frustrated, he threw down his palette and took his brushes to the sink, where he shook them vigorously under the running tap before thrusting them, bristles down, into a mason jar of turpentine. He decided to take himself to a movie. The cool darkness of the theater, he told himself, would distract him enough to return to his work with a fresh perspective. So he made his way through the broiling snarl of Houston traffic to the interior of the air-conditioned mega-plex. Sweat cooled on his neck and arms, and the smell of buttered popcorn trailed him down the hall past bright, noisy video games to the door that matched the number on his ticket.

The film he'd chosen was about a serial killer who was blackmailed into taking on an apprentice. After several unlikely plot twists, the killer wound up framing the apprentice for a murder committed by his daughter. A depressing film, thought David, not only because of its subject matter, but also because of the director's obvious attempt to weave the sort of plot that Hitchcock had constructed with so much more flair and precision. Not surprisingly, the theater was nearly deserted, but when the lights came up after the show, there was the old man's white head a few rows in front of him, tipped up to watch the credits scroll down the screen.

David hadn't seen him come in. He was unnerved to think that the stranger had been so close to him in the dark. Pulling himself roughly out of his seat, David hurried down the lighted steps toward the exit.

THE STRANGER'S CURIOUS, persistent presence in his life became a private joke, something David laughed at to keep his growing uneasiness at bay. Believing himself alone, unobserved at some errand, he'd spot the shuffling figure in the corner of his eye stepping awkwardly toward an empty park bench or sitting in the back of a cab idling at a red light. This continued, and David felt the world around him begin to fray and unravel. When he had a chance to get out of town for the weekend, he jumped at it, hoping that a change of scene would break the spell that held him, enigmatically, in its grip.

An old friend, a painter who had once been his teacher, had an opening at a gallery in a quaint Texas town an hour or so north of Houston. David relished the feeling there of stepping out of time, and the wash of pine shadow flowing over the row of nineteenth-century storefronts, the cafes and galleries and the ice cream parlor on the corner, helped sustain the illusion of escape, as well as mitigating, slightly, the punishing summer heat. That night, his former teacher argued that painting needs to interpret *this* world, and that David was wasting his talent. This was an old debate between them, and David enjoyed renewing it; it took his mind off the clownish, shabby old man dogging his steps. Lying at night on the couch in his teacher's studio, David listened to the sound of crickets in the dark, sunk in a quiet that felt like meditation, devoid of any unwelcome visitors. Before he left on Monday morning, he stopped at the gallery and bought one of his friend's new paintings—a bend in a river overhung with brilliant trees—hoping to take a little serenity back to town with him.

As he approached the outskirts of the city, it was almost noon, and the early lunch traffic began to snarl his progress. Passing one the innumerable strip centers that lined the highway, David noticed a sign for Ace Hardware and decided to stop. His parents were coming to visit in a few months, and he needed to make them a key. There was no rush, of course, but David wanted to extend for as long as possible his interlude of peace and travel, the feeling of freedom it gave him, so he pulled off, parked, and headed across the macadam lot for the entrance.

Inside were long, high-ceilinged rows labeled with hanging signs, a cathedral of brooms and garden tools, ladders and plumbing fixtures, boxes of oily-smelling three- and six-penny nails. David strolled the aisles, breathing in the aroma of lumber and potting soil. He wasn't familiar with the store, but then the harsh, grinding sound of a machine cutting the metal teeth of a key directed his steps. Rounding a corner at the back of a row of deadbolts, he saw something that stopped him as if he'd been slapped.

There was the stranger, his nemesis. The locksmith in a red apron slipped a new silver key into a tiny manila envelope and placed it in the old man's palm. The man grinned at the locksmith, a loose, rubbery smile, the whole time watching David covertly out of the corners of his bloodshot eyes.

Suddenly cold, David swung around and rushed out. But once in his car, in the humid city afternoon with people in the lot and traffic passing on the feeder road, he felt grounded again, at home in a world he recognized and understood. He decided to wait for the old man to come out. He would trail him then and find out who he was; he had to have a name, an address, a job, a credit history. David knew that if he could discover the man's identity, he'd rob the stooped, bleary figure of the hold he exerted on his imagination.

So he waited: fifteen minutes, half an hour. Running his engine for the air-conditioner, David kept his eyes locked on the exit, but the old man never emerged from the store. Finally, he turned off the ignition and went reluctantly back in, walking along the registers and checking each aisle in turn. He expected, at any moment, to come across the unkempt white head, the rumpled khaki shorts hanging at his bony hips, the thin white legs and ridiculous sandals with black socks. But the old man wasn't there.

"I THINK HE'S stalking me."

Nina placed a glass of iced tea on a napkin in front of him and settled into her chair to listen. She was a metal sculptor, and tiny white scars from hot sparks marked her brown arms like constellations. Her thick dark hair was tied back in a faded red handkerchief, and she wore a sleeveless white undershirt under a pair of men's denim overalls.

"Now why would you think *that*, David?"

The plantation shutters in her parlor were slanted against the evening sun, lending the room a shadowy, underwater feel. A ceiling fan whisked the air over their heads. David watched a drop of condensation slide down his glass and darken the napkin.

"Because he's everywhere I go!" Frustrated, he ran his fingers through his mass of black curls. "I never see him come in, and I never see him leave, but when I look up, there he is. I think he *wants* me to see him."

"What on earth for?"

A car drove by in the street, its tires crunching over gravel. When he didn't respond, she added, "He probably just lives near you, and he's on a similar schedule. So he goes to the same places to shop and eat. Really, David, you're making too much of this!"

"Then how do you explain my seeing him in the hardware store this afternoon? I've never been in that place before in my life. And it's miles from where I live!"

Nina shrugged. "Coincidence."

David had been telling himself that same thing for weeks now, and the explanation had worn paper-thin. He'd known Nina Guerrero since art school, and he'd often relied on her before to keep him earth-bound. But this time she was wrong. There was something strange, something terribly *unlikely*, about the way he kept encountering the man, and the more the experience repeated, the more uncanny it became. David wasn't a mathematician, so he had no idea how to calculate the odds against seeing someone so often, in different places and at different times, in a city the size of Houston, but he figured they must be enormous.

And worse, there was something absolutely inexplicable in the way the old man kept appearing without arriving, leaving without going. David looked across at his friend, holding her dark brown eyes with his green stare.

"I don't like it," he said.

Nina smiled and leaned forward, teasing him. "He's a frail old man, right? What do you think he's going to *do* to you?"

That's what David wanted to know.

WHEN HE WAS a grad student, David had taken a job at one of the big hotels downtown to help pay for his art supplies. He'd worked the night shift as a banquet houseman, breaking down the room set-up when a meeting ended, carrying out tables and stacks of chairs, then setting up the space for whatever function was scheduled for the morning. Walking those lighted corridors at night, often alone, the idea had struck him: a hotel is a world in itself. Careers began and ended in seminar rooms, wedding receptions marked new beginnings, and secret affairs unfolded in dimly lit cocktail lounges.

And now, as David's series of strange encounters continued, that world seemed like a welcome refuge. He couldn't afford to leave town just now, but he *could* vanish in another way. Smiling to himself, David packed a bag and booked a room at the Doubletree on Post Oak. He didn't expect his strategic retreat to solve his problem, but he needed a respite, a little time to recover his shattered equilibrium. Twenty minutes later, with his key card in hand and a black canvas suitcase at his feet, David Wilkins rode the glass elevator to his room on the fifth floor, watching the afternoon bustle recede in the lobby below him. He had dinner that evening in the hotel restaurant, then found a seat at the bar in the lounge. The German beer he ordered was poured ceremoniously, perfectly, into a tall Pilsner glass, and he settled back to listen to the singer, a slinky brunette in a silver cocktail dress, as she crooned her way through a medley of jazz standards. Watching her sway seductively in the blue spotlight, David told himself that it was 1961, and that at any moment Sinatra and his cronies would burst through the door in their beautiful suits and thin ties.

Before long the seat next to David at the bar was occupied by a young woman in a shimmering satin blouse. Her name, she informed him, was Nancy Morehouse; she was in sales and in town for a few days on business. With her neat brown bob and doe eyes, she was pretty in a wholesome, Midwestern way, and the extra button open on her cream-colored blouse, one more than usual, told him she was looking for adventure. So he bought her a drink. Casual encounters with strangers were not David's forte, far from it, but he was in need of distraction and didn't believe in refusing the gifts that life sometimes drops at one's feet. They moved from beer to shots of tequila, and shortly thereafter, David found himself tangled in the sheets of salesperson Nancy's king bed in her room on the seventh floor. She'd removed her blouse and skirt, as well as the lacy things beneath them, but, to David's surprise and delight, not her pumps.

I'd like to paint her like that, he thought. She was a whole new kind of angel.

At six-fifteen in the morning, David made his way unsteadily from the elevator down the carpeted hall to his room. Dawn leaked in from a window at the end of the passage, mixing with the green-shaded nightlights burning on the wall to create an otherworldly glow. But David hardly noticed. Despite the beginning of a hangover throbbing at his temples, he felt at home again in his skin. He slipped his magnetic key card into the slot in his door, heard the lock spin open, and pulled down on the handle.

Then another sound made him turn.

The door to the room behind him, just over his shoulder, had opened a crack. The old man's face peered out at him from above the brass door chain: a single blue eye, half a crescent moon of that loose, loony grin. David froze, the door handle cold in his hand.

The moment went on for far too long, but at last the door shut with a soft *click*, releasing him. David packed and left the hotel as fast as he could.

FOR THE NEXT FEW DAYS, he didn't see the man. Those days turned into a week, then two, and August gave way to September. The light was less direct now, and the dusty edges of the live oaks lining Montrose Boulevard began to curl, a sign that the season was changing. David began to think that his bewildering siege was over. Perhaps, he told himself, it had been merely a function of the brutal Houston summer, of too much sun and humidity. He considered how to integrate what had happened into his life, turning it over and over like an oddly shaped piece of a jigsaw puzzle that didn't seem to fit.

One morning at work, he stood on the escalator, a mug of coffee steaming in his hand as the stairs swept him up toward the high white ceiling with its recessed skylights. He had a long, arduous day in front of him, taking down and crating up a show that had run its course, so before he started, he needed a quiet moment to himself. At such times, he would focus on a particular painting he wanted to see, standing in front of it to take it in as he drank his coffee. There were hardly any visitors in the museum at that hour, and the chance to be alone with a masterpiece, the sense of privilege this afforded him, was one of the things David Wilkins like most about his job.

That morning, he wanted to see the Bonnard, the largest of the three in the museum's collection. Inside the frame, a vanity table stood washed in light, and reflected in the mirror above the table was the painter's wife and model, Marthe, newly emerged from her bath, the light gleaming on her wet skin. Frames within frames, like a series of Chinese boxes opening on a secret: the artist's Muse and her dachshund seated on the daybed as the morning sun flooded the room.

Arriving at the top of the escalator, David stepped past the intricately painted Egyptian mummy cases with their winged and jackal-headed gods. He paused briefly to observe, through his pale reflection in the glass, a mummy portrait from Roman times: a young woman stared back at him from death with her olive-colored eyes, a bird perched to sing on her hand. Turning away, David moved through the doorway marked *Modern European Painting* and walked slowly through each gallery, savoring his approach—past Cézanne's hillside in the summer heat, past a windmill by Monet reflected in water, past Van Gogh's swirling, flame-like cypresses and Degas' Russian dancers lifting their knees. He felt as if he were slipping down the narrowing chambers of a telescope toward the eyepiece, the space there concentrated, dense. Ahead of him, he knew, through the next doorway and around the corner to his right, the brilliant, light-washed Bonnard hung waiting.

There was a slight waver in the air, a sense of approaching disclosure. David paused for a moment, then stepped through the open doorway.

Stunned, he found a familiar figure blocking his view: the same blue polo shirt and rumpled shorts, the white hair on the back of the man's head in twisted disarray, as if he'd struggled through a wind tunnel to stand there. The mug David was carrying shattered when it hit the floor, and black coffee spread over the polished marble. His knees buckled, and for an instant it seemed as if the walls of the room were closing in to crush him. But then he steeled himself. The man was playing some kind of perverse game, even if David couldn't begin to fathom what the rules were, and he wanted it to stop. Taking a deep breath, he approached his tormentor and tapped him on the shoulder.

The bland face swung around in response. "Oh," he said, smiling up at David in mock innocence, "it's *you*. I was wondering when you'd get around to speaking to me."

"What do you want? Why are you following me?"

"I was here first. How do you know you're not following me?"

David studied the face before him, the half-smile that implied some secret barely withheld. Broken veins mapped the nose and the corners of his mouth; it was the face of a man with a close and long-standing association with a bottle of Scotch. David wondered if he'd done the right thing in confronting him. He was suddenly sure he was talking to a lunatic.

"Who *are* you?" he asked. "What are you doing here?"

"I might very well ask you those same things, young man."

The depth in the room collapsed, and the stranger's form, impossibly flat and close in the altered space, seemed outlined in fire. David felt his hold on reality slip. He blinked, gripping his head in one hand as he tried to steady himself.

"Good God!" he muttered.

"That's sometimes a misconception," the man put in with a sly smile. "Ever read Job? God's a joker. Take it from me." His eyes blazed suddenly, piercing, magisterial, the features transformed as if they were carved in stone. *"And he sure as hell doesn't care about your level of mental comfort!"*

At that instant, David heard the low rumble of thunder beyond the plaster walls of the museum, and his scalp tightened with awe. But the moment passed as swiftly as it had come, and he again found himself staring at the familiar, bleary grin, the room restored to its normal proportions.

"Look at her!" The old man nodded past David's shoulder as if nothing had happened. "She thinks you're talking to yourself!"

He turned to regard a middle-aged woman in a tailored gray suit watching him from across the room. Seeing herself observed, the woman clutched at her purse and swung briskly into an adjoining gallery, looking once over her shoulder as she hurried away. David heard her heels striking the floor, the hollow sound receding into the empty rooms. For a moment, he was taken aback, but then he realized that any woman, a woman by herself without a lot of people around, would've retreated in the face of the strained glare he'd fixed on her.

He looked back in time to see his adversary slip wordlessly through the doorway.

Pursuing the man out to the second-floor mezzanine, David was surprised at how quickly the gap had opened between them. The white-haired figure moved across the gleaming marble foyer with his familiar shuffling gate, but strangely, he'd covered the distance faster than a much younger man could've done. David wanted to collar the man, to shake him, to get a straight answer after years of silence. *"Wait!"* he called out, but by the time he'd reached the top of the escalator, the old man was already in the hall below, weaving like a pale flame past the statues of Roman gods as he headed for the street. David hurried after him, the thunder barreling again, closer now. But when he pushed through the glass doors and rushed out onto the sidewalk, his quarry was nowhere in sight.

David experienced a moment of eerie dislocation. Then, striding to the corner, he spotted the rumpled figure across the street, standing a half a block away in front of the entrance to the sculpture garden. At first, David thought he was going to duck into the walled, shady enclave, but when he knew he'd been seen, the old man smiled, raised a hand in greeting, and stepped away toward the far intersection. Keeping his eyes on him, David wove through traffic stalled at the light and hurried in pursuit. His feet crunched something brittle on the sidewalk, and glancing down as he passed, he saw the carapaces of insects that had struggled up from the ground and risen into the trees.

When David reached the corner, the old man was fifty yards ahead of him, hobbling along on Montrose Boulevard, head lowered, toward a dark wall of rain sweeping down the street from the north. A spike of lightning branched across the blackened sky. The rain had already obliterated the highway overpass in the distance, and the man rushed toward the storm as if there were wings on his shuffling feet. As David watched, sprinting full speed over the sidewalk in pursuit, the figure was swallowed up in the downpour. David felt the cool air and smelled the rain, and then he felt the torrent stinging his face and arms. But the old man was nowhere to be seen. Though he searched the street for a hundred yards through the driving rain, peering into alleys and even trying locked doors that might've provided an escape, David found no further trace of his adversary.

DAVID WILKINS WAS RELIEVED, at first, that the old man was out of his life. The stranger's assumption of understanding, of an ungranted intimacy, was a burden David was glad to escape. But as the weeks went by, he caught himself watching for his oddly reticent stalker, disappointed not to find the familiar white head and slumped shoulders waiting for him when he entered a café or a store. Eating in a restaurant with friends, he found himself turning from the conversation to watch the door, and when he went to use the men's room, he'd check under every stall, expecting to find a pair of skinny legs terminating in black socks and sandals, the pair of rumpled shorts around his ankles. It was as if some crazy but fascinating relative had died, taking his bizarre theories and insights with him. David's world became smaller.

And he had dreams sometimes when the old man's eyes blazed and the sky cracked and rattled with thunder . . .

Finally, he began doing the only thing he *could* do: looking for a way to put the old man into his paintings. David felt that the door had indeed been opened to him, but not in the way he'd expected, and he had trouble assimilating what had come through. Now he needed to understand what the stranger's presence in his life had meant. Tentatively at first, he began rendering the world he knew, trying to give shape to the glimpse he felt he'd had—cafés and coffee shops in Montrose, bookstores with their shelves reaching to the ceiling, or the long, fluorescent-lighted aisles of a neighborhood grocery with its stacked cans and boxes. The old man was never the subject, never in the center of the painting, always at the edge, half in and half out of the picture. He became the signature in David's work, a presence stepping into or out of the air, implying something beyond the frame, beyond the place where the eye stops.

In the Butterfly House

Anyone watching from the top of the stairs that led to Paul Berryman's studio would've seen the painter arrested at his easel, the brush angled like a weapon in his hand. A gold ring in his left ear gleamed in the morning sunlight, but it was his rapt attention, a certain fixed intent in his expression, which would've drawn and held an observer's notice. His meticulously trimmed black beard was touched with white at the corners of his down-turned mouth, and his close-cropped hair seemed to draw back slightly, enlarging his forehead as he scrutinized his work.

The walls of his studio were covered with tacked-up sketches, dozens of them, some in charcoal and some in pencil, all of them versions of the image he studied so fixedly on the easel before him. It was a portrait of sorts, but unlike any he'd attempted before, the woman's body broken as if she'd fallen from a great height. The subject was a pale, icy blonde named Allison Reese he'd meet in the park.

Gray eyes stared back at him from the canvas. Riveted, he laid the brush down carefully on his work table, keeping his gaze on hers.

He'd first met Allison Reese along the bayou where he went to run. When his eye fell on her, she smiled at him—just polite recognition—but he was thunderstruck. Her blonde hair, so fair it was nearly white and fine as a child's, fell forward over her face as she leaned to tighten the laces of her running shoes, and the eyes that met his, peering out from the pale shadow of that hair, were a colorless smoke-gray, cool and acute. Later, he tried to analyze the effect she'd had on him. Maybe it was her pallor, the impression she created of living marble, or the nearly perfect symmetry of her features. Whatever the reason, Allison Reese was the most fascinating woman Berryman had seen in a long time. There was something ethereal about her, something that attracted and unnerved him, and he knew he had to paint her.

And that meant sleeping with her first, of course.

The following morning, he'd gone to the park intending to make his move. If her ring finger were bare, he would ask her out to dinner; if not, he would invite her to have coffee with him. Married women usually preferred such games, at least initially, even if they knew damn well that a man wanted to go to bed with them. He would turn on the charm, give her some time to get comfortable with him, and then take her to bed. After that, he would ask her to sit for him. Berryman had done this many times before, and he had yet to meet a woman who was not flattered to be painted, especially once they knew his reputation.

So when his own run was finished, he lingered near the bench, deliberately turned away, feigning nonchalance. The Gulf breeze cooled the sweat on his neck and shoulders. Glancing behind him, he saw a pale shape approaching from the dark wall of pines, knees lifting, the arms pumping for speed. He heard steps at his back, labored breathing. Berryman readied himself and swung around to face her.

She stood regarding him, hands on the hips of her black bicycle shorts, a cropped white tee shirt. The directness of her gaze unsettled him, and the artist controlled with an effort his impulse to step back or look away. Even dripping with sweat, she was lovely. Five four, he guessed, her chest heaving with exertion.

"Good run?" he asked.

"Not bad," she breathed. "I like running in the morning."

"Me, too. It always clears my head. Sets me up for a good day's work."

"What do you do?"

Those eyes had not left his. The game was on.

"I put paint on blank canvases and try to convince people to buy them."

"Does that ever work?"

"Sometimes," he shrugged, letting her hear the understatement in his response. His work was selling well these days, and Berryman knew there wasn't a woman alive who didn't respond to money, regardless of what she might claim. His eyes traveled over her. The run had put a shine on her skin, like marble stroked with a wet sponge.

"Like what you see?" she asked.

"Yes," he replied simply, meeting her gaze.

A light came into her eyes, and she regarded him in silence—feral, predatory. But she had it backwards. She was the rabbit; he was the goddamn wolf. He would make certain she understood that. Stepping toward her, he held out his hand.

"I'm Paul Berryman."

She grasped the hand, her fingers like ice, the grip surprisingly strong. "Allison Reese," she said. The sun, flashing from behind the glass skyline of Houston as it climbed the humid morning air, threw a spotlight on them. The magnolias cast long shadows on the grass. To Berryman's left, the muddy roll of Buffalo Bayou made a low, nearly inaudible rumble as it slid around a bend past a stand of pines. He asked her to dinner, suggesting an Italian place he knew on a back street off Montrose, very intimate, with a decent wine list.

She regarded him in silence for a moment. "Okay," she agreed, her smile equally faint, suggestive, dangerous. "You asked for it."

Berryman suppressed the urge to slap her, hard, to set things straight. He knew she was teasing him, coaxing him on, and as his gaze slipped over her trim white form, the swell of her breasts and hips, he felt a warm stir in his groin. He imagined slamming her against the wall of his studio, ripping her blouse, taking her.

"Seven okay?"

She gave him her address.

AT DINNER THAT NIGHT, Berryman studied the woman across from him. Candlelight played across her features, casting a gleam on the bridge of her perfect nose, making her gray eyes larger, moving shadows over the curved line of her cheek.

"I'm a homicide cop," she replied.

"You're kidding me."

When he'd asked what she did for a living, he had not expected that. Still, in a way, it fit. Throughout dinner, he'd plied her with the usual conversation designed to impress—places he'd traveled, unusual things that had happened to him there—and she'd sat silent, smiling faintly, as if she understood perfectly well what he was up to and was enjoying the performance. She evaluated him as if he were a suspect she already knew was guilty.

The murmur of conversation at other tables filled the momentary silence.

"Oh yes," she sighed. "I've seen a lot of dead bodies."

The artist wondered, at first, if he'd heard her right.

"A corpse has no pretensions," she added, unfazed. "All the nonsense has been stripped away, all the little lies we tell ourselves. And other people." Her gaze, lifted to his, was an accusation. "There's a faraway look on a dead man's face. If you get to him soon enough—before the eyes cloud over."

Berryman was appalled, but fascinated. How could a woman say such things with a smile on her face? For a moment, he couldn't form a response. Not a right one, anyway.

"You like catching a murderer, putting him away?"

She snickered derisively. "To tell you the truth, I could care less. I like the hunt, but I don't give a damn about public safety. As far as I'm concerned, citizens should learn to take care of themselves. I'm not the public's daddy."

No, he could see she wasn't. "Then why do you do it?"

Her grin widened, the nearest thing he'd seen all night to enthusiasm. The waiter arrived to clear dinner, and she beamed up at the white-jacketed young man with ironic sweetness. He stepped off with their plates.

"To catch a killer," she responded, when they were alone again, "you have to think like a killer. I like that. I'm *good* at it. I relish going to that place in my mind. I'd do the work for nothing if they'd let me."

Not for the first time that evening, Berryman wondered if he he'd made a mistake asking this woman out. The face across from his was a mask: white porcelain, bland and flawless. Only the eyes stared out at him, shining with a cold intent he couldn't decipher. Still, he was intrigued, and the undercurrent of danger only increased his curiosity, his appetite. As his eyes touched the pearls lying at her throat and followed the plunge of the black cocktail dress between her breasts, the last of his doubt and reluctance evaporated.

He recognized this woman: like him, she was a predator.

"Why did you agree to go out with me tonight?" he asked.

She lifted the glass balloon, swirling the last of the old Barolo he'd ordered, the wine so dark it was nearly black, a flash of red where the candle flame reflected.

"You remind me of a man I spent some time with."

"A lover?" Berryman ventured. Her fingernails were red, as dark as the wine in the half-light.

"That's a stupid euphemism." She drank from her glass. "A man who fucked me. The only one who ever had the guts to do it right. I spent some time in his cellar. I'm not sure how long, really. Time seemed to stop." She impaled him with her blank, colorless eyes, and he thought for a moment that her mask would shatter into twenty pieces. "All the boundaries I kept between myself and the world were torn down—you understand? I didn't know where I stopped and everything else began. It was devastating, terrifying—*wonderful*. The most transforming experience I've ever had."

That twinge of fear mixed with excitement was new. He liked it. "Sounds great," he managed, his voice thick.

She drained her glass and leaned forward, eyeing him, her elbows on the white linen tablecloth. Candlelight played across her forehead and cast the rest of her face in shadow.

"You talk the talk," she said. "But can you walk the walk?"

Berryman snapped his credit card on the table and signaled for the waiter. Moments later, just beyond the string of lights that marked the entrance, he pressed himself against her, his heart slamming in his chest, breathing in her perfume in the warm fall night as the valet ran for his car. His hand wandered down her thigh.

"Not here," she smiled.

A few stars glinted coldly in the black boughs of a live oak. Berryman helped her into the bucket seat of his Jaguar, his glance sliding over her bare legs. A short drive north on Montrose, past the usual grey ghosts in raincoats haunting the bus stops, took them to his place. There was a momentary pause as the electric gate on his driveway rolled open; then he ushered her to the back door and into his dimly lit kitchen.

Berryman led her upstairs to his studio, the smell of turpentine stinging his nose. When he switched on the overhead lights, his Lorelei sprang out of the shadows.

Wordlessly, his dinner guest drifted toward the paintings, her head cocked slightly to one side. She was fascinated, and the glow of pride the artist felt diverted, for the moment, his more immediate intentions. He was gathering work for an exhibition that would open in a few days, and his obsession spoke silently, eloquently, from the walls. She stood in the middle of the room, turning slowly to take in the images that surrounded her. When she completed the circle, her eyes returned to a picture in the corner. She glided toward it slowly, pulled by invisible strings, her back to him, not speaking.

The canvas showed a pale nude, a redhead, squatting with her back to a wall, her arms pinioned over her head, hands bound with a rope that rose out of the picture frame. It was the woman's frank expression, more than her vulnerability, which gave the piece its power to disturb. The face stared out at the viewer, accusing, implicating.

Berryman stepped up behind her. "What do you think?" he breathed at her ear.

Without warning, she swung around and slapped him hard across the face, stunning him with the speed of her attack. She fixed him with a livid glare, pointing at the canvas, her mask down at last. "How *dare* you," she whispered. The bound woman gazed out at them.

Her arm drew back again, fist balled shut, and Berryman jerked his head aside, narrowly avoiding the blow. Before he could react, she sprang on him, driving her shoulder into his chest, knocking him off balance. She dug her nails into his face, ripping the flesh, and when he raised an arm to block another punch, she drove her knee into his groin.

Pain and anger exploded in his skull. He managed to get hold of her arm and heave her across the room. She hit the wall with one shoulder and slid to her knees.

Crouching on all fours, Allison Reese turned to meet his furious, uncomprehending stare. "You're dead," she pronounced, her voice like ice. "*Dead*."

The artist snatched a hammer from his work table and lunged toward her, clumsy with pain, his movements thick and slow. He could feel the blood wet on his face, and he was enraged enough at that instant to bash her brains out. And something more: he was deliriously excited. If he could've gotten his hands on her, he would've smashed her against the wall and taken her by force. He wanted to bruise her, to hear her scream.

Dodging away, she slipped down the stairs laughing, and he heard the front door slam before he'd closed half the distance between them. Berryman reached the door and peered out through the transom to see her facing him on the lawn. She smiled at him tightly, decidedly; then lifted her arms, hands joined as if she had a gun, and pumped two imaginary bullets into his head. She turned and ran, her black dress merging with the night. Disembodied white arms and legs moved off into darkness.

Her white-blonde hair, ruffled in a breeze, was the last thing he saw before she vanished. He thought of a match struck in a black, empty room.

BERRYMAN FIGURED he'd seen the last of Allison Reese. It was clear to him that the woman he'd taken to dinner was disturbed, caught up in some brittle, dangerous way with the kind of images he painted. Though his work had nothing to do with her, she had obviously taken it personally. He supposed he should be flattered. But he resolved to be more circumspect in his choice of potential companions in the future.

Two nights later, near midnight, the artist returned home after the opening of his new exhibition. He'd sold five paintings—a year's expenses in a single night!—and he'd surely sell a few more before the show closed. The rich liked his work: they had decided he was daring, and his canvases had begun to grace the private drawing rooms of shaded brick houses in River Oaks and Memorial and on North Boulevard. Sighing wearily, he tossed his keys to the kitchen table, relishing the dark silence of the house, when a flash of broken glass on the floor caught his eye. He stared at it, not comprehending, at first, what he was seeing. Then a shadow detached itself from the corner and stepped menacingly toward him.

Black jeans and boots, her face and hair colorless above a black sweater, her eyes gleaming like grey ice. A pair of handcuffs dangled from the index finger of the hand she raised toward him. Her smile was a threat, and though Berryman understood at once that he was in danger, an eerie sensation of dreaming stole over him at her sudden, soundless appearance.

"Want to play?" she whispered, jangling the cuffs. "Got the nerve?"

The words brought him back to himself. Snatching the phone from its charger, Berryman backed out of the kitchen, punching *9-1-1*. She drifted after him, laughing, and tossed the handcuffs on the dining room table.

"Really Paul, I thought you had more guts. I thought you were an explorer."

Glancing up, he saw an automatic pistol aimed at his head, and his heart raced with a sudden rush of panic. "Give me that phone," she demanded. He handed it to her.

"Good boy." She pressed the off button just as the operator came on. "Now let's go into the parlor, shall we? I'll think we'll be more comfortable there."

Switching the Beretta to her other hand, she leaned forward to run her fingers lightly over the wounds in his face. The painter's fear balanced wildly on an upsurge of anger; he couldn't believe this was happening.

"Put these on your ankles," she told him, grabbing the handcuffs from the table and tossing them at him. Berryman caught them against his chest.

His mind worked, searching for some escape. Then he felt the gun barrel cold against his forehead. "*Do it*," she crooned.

He sat rigid in a straight-backed wooden chair, the cuffs on his ankles, his wrists bound in front of him with a length of rope. She'd taken down a hanging plant and smashed the clay pot against the wall, threading the rope through the hook in the ceiling so she could work it, work *him*, like a marionette. Now he watched as she undressed, slowly, meticulously, folding her clothes and laying them neatly on the couch. She straddled him, pulling down hard on the rope so his arms rose over his head. The hand that held the rope also held a switchblade to his throat, and she warned him not to move as she applied the make-up to his face with her free hand: the thick white foundation, dark red lipstick, the midnight-blue eye shadow she smeared over his eyelids with the ball of her thumb. Different emotions flared up and mixed in Berryman—fear, humiliation, furious anger that she could *use* him like this. A sense of unreality crept over him, but every time, the point of the knife at his throat and those cold gray eyes, insistent, inches from his own, brought him back to what was happening. She made him into a whore, a doll, something inhuman, something you could do with as you pleased.

"Keep still, you *bitch*," she whispered at one ear.

At that instant, the knife lifted briefly from his throat, and Berryman saw his chance. He stood, heaving her violently from his lap. She landed hard on her hands and knees, the switchblade in her fist, the little tubes and jars of makeup scattering noisily across the floor. Desperately, unthinkingly, Berryman threw himself on her—he heard a sharp, wheezing intake of breath and understood at once what had happened.

Struggling awkwardly to his feet, he looked down at her.

The knife had buried itself in the left side of her throat. She was choking, suffocating on her own blood. Berryman rushed for the phone, hands tied, and clumsily punched the buttons to call for an ambulance.

He yanked out the blade, then grabbed her sweater from the pile of clothes on the couch and pressed it against the wound, trying to stop the bleeding. Her eyes pierced him, the pupils contracted to pinpoints. She was going into shock: he could feel her skin getting colder as he kneeled in the blood. When the ambulance arrived, the artist was standing over her with his weirdly painted face, entranced, a length of rope trailing from his pinioned wrists. He stared down at the white form prone at his feet like a smashed lily, limbs splayed, her lifeblood seeping out over his polished hardwood floor . . .

After, there had been questions asked again and again by the police, the same questions repeated at the grand jury hearing. "Were you intimate with Allison Reese?" they'd all wanted to know.

"Only at knife point," he'd told them.

"Did you mean to kill her?"

"No." But he was relieved that she was dead. She'd turned him into one of the women he painted, and he hated her for that.

Listening to testimony in the crowded grand jury room, Berryman discovered that Detective Sergeant Allison Reese had been found shackled to the cellar wall of a man she'd been investigating, a serial killer who had eluded capture for months. The police psychiatrist who'd examined her after her ordeal had insisted that she be suspended and put on permanent disability. According to the psychiatrist, she'd been repeating what she'd endured, trying to control the experience, to relive it but change the outcome.

No charges were filed against Berryman.

He started dreaming about her then. He saw her pale form circling the house, alternately flaring in the moonlight and vanishing in shadow. She clawed at the doors and windows like an animal, trying to get in. He'd wake with a start, knowing that sleep was out of the question, doggedly climb the stairs to his studio, and snatch up his pad, working quickly, making sketch after sketch in the four a.m. stillness. At such times, he felt the silence in the rooms at the bottom of the stairwell lapping like black water at the edge of his awareness, a slowly rising tide, and he worked with a frantic sense of urgency.

Now he stood in front of his easel, arms folded across his chest, considering.

On the canvas, Allison Reese sprawled naked, inverted and prone on the floor, her head toward the bottom of the picture. Her splayed limbs formed a broken cross, and a shining ribbon of blood flowed from her throat. Hanging down, her hair fanned out, a halo of white fire, and her eyes, ecstatic and reproving, impaled the viewer like the eyes of an angel in a Byzantine icon.

The habit of critical removal from his work was an old one. Pleased, Berryman decided that he'd finally gotten the translucent quality of her skin right. "*Got you!*" he muttered to himself. "You belong to me now."

But his words made him uneasy.

WHITE AUTUMN SUNLIGHT danced over the walls of the studio. A breeze trailed in through the open window, rustling the drawings. Berryman felt heavy, submerged. For days, he'd gone without sleep as he struggled to capture the image in his mind. Now he could afford to rest. He stretched out on the couch across the room and closed his eyes.

Silence, an underwater ringing in his ears—

She stepped from the canvas and stood across the paint-spattered floor, regarding him, the wet blood gleaming at her throat. As she walked toward him, he rose from the couch, stunned, disbelieving: her progress was deliberate but slow, unhurried, the light sliding on her hips. He wanted desperately to get away, but unaccountably, his steps moved toward her one by one, closing the distance between them. She lifted her hands to him, and he saw that they were bound, the wrists looped together and knotted with a heavy cord. He found there was a knife in his hand, and against his will, he began sawing at the rope, watching the strands fray and part. She smiled at him, impatient, a hungry, predatory expression on her dead face . . .

Berryman woke with a sharp intake of breath. A sense of her arrival, impending at any instant, spun in the sun-motes that fell through his window. He needed to get out of the house.

Fifteen minutes later, he parked in the circle of spaces surrounding the bronze statue of Sam Houston on horseback. Emerging from his Jaguar, Berryman made his way past a row of yellow school buses, through the crowd of children trailing helium balloons and scattering popcorn from paper bags to pigeons colored and streaked like a rainy day. Harried teachers and parents shouted commands the distracted children ignored, the pigeons rustling and cooing and more of them arriving with a clapping of wings out of the late-morning air.

Berryman passed through the glass doors of the Museum of Natural History and paid his entrance fee at the counter. The children who followed him in ran screaming for the bones of a Tyrannosaurus rex that stalked through the room to his right, but the artist stepped quickly along the corridor behind them, heading for the Cockrell Butterfly Center. He wanted to sit in the rainforest beneath the glass dome, listening to the sound of falling water while those bright creatures flickered around him, wanted to sit still enough for one to land on his shoulder with an imperceptible weight. It always calmed him to do that.

Entering the exhibit, he felt the coolness of rock and water on his face. He moved past lighted displays showing the stages of transformation: insects emerging from the shrouds of their papery cocoons and hanging to dry and harden their wings. Then he stepped into the cavern. A waterfall crashed down from thirty feet above, the rock wall hung with moss and orchids, and he began climbing the gradually ascending path to the top of the exhibit.

The air was full of fluttering color. Dozens of butterflies drifted over the profusion of vines and flowers, tracing their circling mazes in the air, their invisible alphabets: monarch, southern belle, blue morpho, lacewing, tiger longwing. A walkway snaked through the dense garden of elephant ears and hanging vines. There was a sweet, rotten smell of fruit. A cloud of butterflies swarmed over the chunks of papaya and kiwi left out for them to feed on.

His ears registered the dull roar of the waterfall, its mist blurring the boundaries of objects. The people strolling past him, distracted by the wings in the air, seemed to exist in another world. From beneath a stone bench, an impassive iguana eyed him.

Stepping slowly through the mist and flickering color, Berryman kept his eyes on a space ahead of him where the path turned. It was dense with butterflies: gold rim, malachite, banded orange. They lighted on something that wasn't there, outlining it, flexing their wings, striking a kind of fire; and as more butterflies arrived, drawn from all directions as if some sweet, invisible flower were opening, he could see that there *was* something there—a figure facing away from him, a woman, her arms held out straight from her shoulders and lined with patterned wings.

Slowly, the figure turned, and two gray eyes blinked open out of thin air. Recognition was immediate: there was no mistaking her eyes.

Berryman felt a shock, a sickness so profound at the core of himself that he couldn't command his body. He heard a strangled cry of protest, of negation, and realized only vaguely that it had issued from his own throat. Nauseated, disbelieving, the artist turned and stumbled up the stairs, lurching thickly, urgently, along an ascending pathway and rushing for the exit.

Bursting through a set of doors, he found himself in a darkened room, a maze lined with lighted cases of dead and labeled insects. Another flight down, and Berryman was hurrying past the entrance to other exhibits, his sight fixed on the tinted glass doors that opened to the street. A child who ran in front of him was knocked sprawling to the ground. The mother's outraged scream pursued him into the daylight as the artist sprinted across the pavement and into the green depths of Hermann Park, wanting only to put as much distance as he could between himself and what he'd seen.

Out of breath, Paul Berryman collapsed on a bench in the shade of a live oak. Sunlight wove through the green passages of the tree, flickering its wings over him. One of his bound women had broken her chains and come after him, and he knew there was nowhere in the world he could go now to get away from her. He glanced around wildly, and though the bright day was empty in every direction, he expected, at any moment, to see his white nightmare come gliding toward him across the lush expanse of lawn.

Uncle Edward

"A poet might succumb to the domination of a marionette, for a marionette has only imagination."
—Rainier Maria Rilke

I

The first thing that Isaiah McPhearson noticed when he opened his eyes was the way the sunlight backlit the translucent stretch of canvas overhead. It reminded him of light passing through apple blossoms, and for a moment, he thought he had fallen asleep beneath a tree back home in his orchard; but then the smell of the heated tent and blood and the coughing and shifting of men on cots around him returned him to his circumstances. A picture floated into his brain, a nightmare like an engraving from Doré: three men were holding him down, and a fourth man cut him as he screamed and pleaded with them. He shook the image away and tried to sit up but fell back clumsily to his cot, pain knifing through his shoulder. Then he saw why.

His left arm was gone.

The doctor gave him a bottle of whiskey and told him to drink. While the orderlies held him, the doctor sawed through the flesh and bone and burned the stump to stop the bleeding. And then he remembered the popping sounds, almost innocent, and the thin wisps of smoke coming from the trees until there was nothing but smoke and that manic yodeling as the men in gray and dun ran toward him. He'd felt a burning in his arm and had fallen, believing at first that a horse had kicked him. The minié ball had shattered the bone in his arm, and it hadn't been long before the fever and gangrene had set in. Every soldier in this war knew what that meant.

Gingerly, using the arm that remained, McPhearson sat up and swung his legs to the ground. He saw his white feet in the dust beside his cot—at least he still had two good legs. He struggled into his boots, slipped into a blood-stained white coat thrown over an unused cot, opened the tent flap, and stepped into the daylight.

His legs were weak at first, but the air soon revived him. In every direction, tents reached to the horizon, and McPhearson knew where he was. This makeshift city of suffering had sprung up outside Washington to deal with the maimed and dying that each new battle produced in such numbers. When McPhearson had joined the Army of the Potomac, every officer had assured him that the war would be over in a few weeks, but that was more than three years ago, and still there was no end in sight. In this last engagement, blue bodies had littered the earth, and not an inch of ground had been taken. They'd listened to the dying calling out for water from the mass of corpses, and when his mess-mate, John Keillor, had ventured out with a canteen, a sniper had put a bullet in his brain.

McPhearson wandered, lost in thought, until he came to a tent marked with a wooden sign: *Surgery*. A high-pitched scream pierced the silence, and the hair rose in a cold path over his skull. A jumble of severed limbs lay heaped up in sunlight outside the tent. He approached slowly, a man in a dream, wondering if his own lost arm was in that tangle. Would he recognize it? He gazed down at the legs and arms, asking himself how it would feel to link them, to put a man together instead of taking him apart. He bent down to admire the way an ankle slimmed to its hinge, the beautiful mechanism of knees and elbows, how the fingers of a severed hand curled as if to hold a tool or to cradle an apple.

An idea, fully formed, flooded the soldier's mind. He stood, and again the current sparked down his spine: he knew what to do. If he started walking now, north and a little west, he could be home in five days.

THE FIRST HINTS OF DAWN glowed in the east when Isaiah McPhearson approached the dark shape of the barn, entering silently and finding the axe in its corner. The orchard was old, planted on the site of an Indian massacre, but still bearing fruit. A French-led confederation of Algonquians had raided southeast into British territory one hundred and twenty years ago, and now the roots of these twisted trees clutched dreamless heads and wove through ribcages, the orchard stubbornly yielding its dark fruit every autumn. McPhearson felled a tree, chopped away the smaller branches, and was hacking one-armed at a second trunk when a noise behind him made him turn. It was Charity, his wife. The light was up now, tinted green as it filtered through branches, but she had to stare for several seconds before she recognized the manic stranger in the blood-stained white coat as her husband and threw herself into his embrace. She felt the empty sleeve and pulled away to study his features, so changed, the bones of his face sharpened by suffering.

McPhearson's task obsessed him. He barely spoke at all and flatly refused to discuss his work with anyone. He dragged his cache of apple wood to the barn, where he planed and sawed and hammered with his remaining arm, sometimes laboring deep into the night by the glow of a kerosene lamp. Charity, her brother Jon, and her twelve-year-old son Joshua kept the farm running, but none of them knew what to say when the neighbors came to call, anxious for news, hearing that Isaiah McPhearson was back from the war; and if McPhearson knew that his neighbors believed he was mad, he showed no concern. A limb at a time, he was carving a man from apple wood, assembling the pieces, joints hinged with tiny brass plates, the delicate fingers able to open and close. The mannequin stood nearly six feet tall, eye-level with McPhearson, its sharp cheekbones and hooked nose giving it an expression of fierce intent and concentration. He sanded and polished the wood, rubbing it with linseed oil until it glowed with a ruddy light. Then he attached the strings: he had worked out the pattern on his long walk home, a network of connections as elaborate as thought coursing along the synapses of the brain. No one could imagine how he did it.

McPhearson practiced by the hour in the barn, working the strings from the hayloft, until his wooden man could open and close the doors, pitch hay, and bring the yoke and harness down from their pegs to fit them on the impassive mule. Joshua relayed the story in whispers to a friend, who told another friend, and soon a gaggle of local boys gathered daily at the peephole in the barn wall to take turns watching, open-mouthed, as the puppet strode through the sun-striped shadows.

The boys named the marionette Uncle Edward, and always spoke of him with a mixture of awe and fear, as if he were a living man.

AS THE PUPPET GREW more accomplished, Isaiah McPhearson withered and wasted away.

Finally, seven years after the war had at last ended, his family laid him in the earth among his forebears in a plot of ground at the edge of the orchard.

In his will, McPhearson left a codicil: the marionette's strings were to be cut when he was dead. The family took this as a further sign of his madness, or at best of the isolating jealousy his creation had inspired in him. He wanted no one else to work the strings of his puppet.

But since it cost nothing, the strings were indeed cut, and the wooden man, an embarrassment and painful reminder, was consigned to an unused corner of the barn. Charity's brother Jon continued to work the land. He kept a whiskey still in a thicket along the creek, and he took to hiding a jar of his home-brew in the loft. Late one afternoon in May, the whiskey buzzing in his brain, Jon emerged from the barn to see a dark thunderhead looming over the orchard. The storm approached quickly, blotting out the daylight, turning the air black and purple and green, the smear of a bruise against the white bloom of the orchard. The unstrung marionette sat in a chair at the edge of the trees, his wooden gaze aimed into the branches. Jon felt his anger flare. He guessed immediately what had happened: the local brats had dragged his dead brother-in-law's folly from the barn and propped it there to taunt the family. They had even stolen into the house for a rush-bottomed chair!

Thunder rumbled, and a fine, needling rain began to fall. As Jon watched, the puppet stood and walked into the orchard, vanishing into the streaked tangle of moss and mangled flowers.

II

"HOW LONG HAS IT BEEN since you've seen the place?"

Tom Jamieson answered his wife, Pru, without taking his gaze from the road. "I guess it's been nearly thirty years."

"What do you expect to find? Wrack and ruin, I suppose."

"I doubt it. Grandmother McPhearson always kept the clapboard painted and the hardwoods waxed. When she died, the house went to her sister, my great-aunt Polly." Tom grinned at her quickly and returned his eyes to the highway. "Now there was a crazy old bat! Her red hair stood on end and her eyes were always wide open, as if she'd just stuck her finger in an electric outlet. She looked constantly terrified."

Tom sighed to himself and shook his head, surprised to acknowledge how long it had been since he'd given his mother's eccentric side of the family a thought. He had never told Pru about the McPhearsons. It was not that he'd consciously withheld the information, but these family stories seemed distant, a part of the past far removed from their busy lives in Harrisburg. Tom sometimes worked seventy hours or more a week, the dues an ambitious lawyer is expected to pay if he wants to become a partner, and Pru's paintings were beginning to sell in the local galleries with encouraging regularity. His precursors on his mother's side had always struck Tom as so much cracked china—delicate, ethereal in their translucence, but impractical and profoundly unsuited for the bumps and jarrings of the contemporary world. And indeed, they were all gone now. With Polly's death, the house had come into his hands.

"Sounds like you have some mad relations you've never told me about," Pru grinned at him.

Ever since he had first known her, his wife had possessed an uncanny ability to pick up on his train of thought. She'd demonstrated this so often that it hardly seemed strange anymore.

"The house is haunted, isn't it?" she added suddenly.

Tom glanced across at her, not certain that he wanted to tell her too much. Pru had a mystical, superstitious tendency which, in his opinion, needed no encouragement. Although he hadn't said anything to her about it yet, Tom was toying with the possibility of moving in; living in an historical house in the country like a landed gentleman appealed to him, and it would afford him a certain cachet at the office, as well. It could help him make partner. So he didn't want to plant any ideas in his wife's mind that might germinate.

"Not really," he responded.

"What do you mean, *not really*? Come on," she urged him, punching his arm. "Tell."

The car spun through the early May sunlight, one of those first warm days when the earth releases a fragrance and the grass and trees flame out with original fire. There seemed to be no darkness possible in the world. What harm, he asked himself, could a colorful story do?

"Well, my great-great grandfather, Isaiah McPhearson, fought in the Union army during the Civil War. For most of the war, anyway. One day in 1864, he figured he'd had enough, and he walked home."

"Stubbornness runs in the family," Pru observed.

"I guess. Anyway, he'd lost an arm at Cold Harbor. Lost at least half his mind as well, according to the family. He made a life-size marionette out of wood from the orchard, and he spent the rest of his life working the thing in the barn."

She was intrigued. "Where does the ghost come in?"

"Not a ghost, exactly. Every once in a while, someone sees the puppet move. People have seen it walking."

"What people?"

"Members of the family, mostly."

Pru was silent, staring at him, and Tom could tell she was picturing the man of wood creaking through the house at night. He wished he hadn't told her.

"Just silly family stories," he suggested.

"Why didn't they get rid of the thing?"

"Respect for Isaiah, I imagine. Apparently, he was an impressive man, even if he was crazy. Besides, the doll was a beautiful object, hand-carved, all the whorls and notches of the grain showing."

"You've seen it?"

Him, his mind responded. *I've seen him*.

"Sure. I was only there once, visiting for a few weeks in the summer when I was six. Uncle Edward sat in a chair by the hearth in the front parlor, exactly like a member of the family."

"*Uncle Edward?*" Pru shook her head, and he was relieved to hear her laugh. "My God, the entire family's delusional. What kind of a clan have I married into?" She leaned forward, teasing him with her eyes. "Tell the truth. Did a lot of cousins get married on your mother's side? Brothers and sisters, perhaps?"

"Would you have married me if they had?"

"Probably," Pru responded. "But I would've insisted on a prenuptial agreement."

TOM HAD INDEED SEEN Uncle Edward. He was a link in the bloodline, going back a hundred and forty years or more, which had experienced what he had to assume was a shared hallucination. A man of wood cannot move. But boys have vivid imaginations, and what boy could resist the overwhelming suggestion of a puppet sitting in a parlor as if he were about to speak?

Tom had loved his grandmother's farm. Released from the constraints of the city, he'd run through the barn and orchard like a puppy who had finally broken his chain. He'd spent hours with a group of local boys at an irrigation pond, swinging out on a rope tied to the branch of a sycamore and dropping into the water, shattering the reflection of the tree. He had known the emergence of a buried recognition when animals stepped from the brush and revealed themselves—woodchucks, deer, a quick red fox—creatures he'd only seen before in picture books. On the Fourth of July, he had dashed through the orchard waving his blue sparkler like a shooting star as the green-smelling night closed in on him.

One rainy afternoon, he had accidentally smashed a flour jar in the kitchen. When his grandmother discovered the mess, he told her Uncle Edward had done it. "Ah," she said. "Uncle

Edward." Thereafter, whenever he left something out where it should not be or broke something—as six-year-olds, with their combination of curiosity and clumsiness, sometimes will in a new place—he blamed it on the marionette. This became a family joke, and Uncle Edward's name was invoked again and again. Then, the night before his father was to arrive to take him home, Tom was awakened very late by a powerful crash of thunder that boomed and rolled over the house. A man stood by the bed, and the boy assumed his father had come early. But when a spike of lightning turned the room white, he saw the mannequin gazing down at him. He woke the house with his screaming.

With a boy's instinctive faith in sympathetic magic, he believed that the puppet had come because he'd called it. For months, that fierce expression, all its angles sharpened by the momentary burst of light, haunted his sleep, appearing at his bedside in answer to his unconscious summons. Although he was invited, the boy never returned to his grandmother's farm.

A GRAVEL ROAD WOUND through a profusion of flowering apple trees, the whitened branches humming with bees, and deposited Tom and Pru Jamieson in front of the house. It was a square, two-story structure, white, with a fieldstone foundation and a chimney rising on each side, the roof topped with a glassed-in widow's watch. The house stood on a rise that commanded a view of the rolling landscape planted with fruit trees and green corn.

The door had been left open, so they walked in and found themselves in a long hallway. The pine floors gleamed, time-darkened and softened by many steps, and gave a little, Tom thought, creaking with his weight as they had during that long-ago summer when he was six. Oak doors opened to sitting rooms on both sides of the hall, and in the back of the house, they discovered the kitchen. The fireplace, intended for cooking, was large enough to stand in, and an iron door in the stone hearth opened on an oven for baking bread. Dented copper pots and Dutch ovens, suspended from pegs in the ceiling beams, reflected the May sunlight that traveled in through the wave of hand-blown glass in the windows. A door led downstairs to a cellar with an earthen floor and fieldstone walls, a huge stone in one corner carved with a name and date: *Nathan McPhearson, 1816.* Upstairs, the master bedroom had a fireplace with a thick length of pine for a mantle. The bath contained a claw-footed tub, a separate shower, and two freestanding sinks with mirrors. *His and hers*, he thought. Indoor plumbing and electricity had been added to the house in the sixties, and clearly, everything had been maintained with meticulous care. Tom and Pru found themselves in a back room, the space empty, with a row of windows looking south over white trees and the distant green gouge of a stream.

"This would make a nice studio," he offered.

Pru was silent for a moment, weighing, considering the landscape. "We'll need some rugs and a couch or two. Some of the rooms downstairs are a little austere."

Tom smiled to himself.

A FEW MINUTES LATER, Tom was lingering in the upstairs hall, running his hand lovingly over the woodwork, when his wife's voice reached him.

"There's someone up here!"

Her tone alerted him that something was wrong before her words, muted by the intervening walls, registered. She had opened the door that led up a narrow stair to the widow's watch, and now, as Tom turned to find out what was wrong, he saw her feet backing down the steps, quickly but carefully. In an instant, she faced him.

"Tom, there's someone up there," she repeated. Her eyes were wide.

He climbed the stairs hand over hand, looking up, his voice preceding him. "Hello. Can I help you?"

From where she waited below, Pru could hear his steps cross the room and stop. There was a pause, and then his words spiraled down to her.

"Pru, it's okay, really. Come up here. I want to show you something."

As her head rose into the little room, she saw her husband standing by a man seated in a chair. He waved her forward, and Pru approached to find herself gazing at a profile with a sharply hooked nose. On the figure's knee a hand rested, beautifully shaped and hinged with tiny brass plates, the swirl of grain, she noticed, like fingerprints.

"Uncle Edward?" she asked, looking at Tom.

He nodded.

The puppet stared through the flawed glass at a hillside of flowering trees.

III

SO THE JAMIESONS MOVED IN. Pru, in particular, was a little unnerved by the puppet occupying its glassed-in room like a proprietor, but she soon gave herself over to the process of claiming the house, adding the touches—a chair here, a painting there—that would make the place their own. Taking possession of her studio was especially seductive, and it put her last reservations to rest. The row of southern windows filled the room with light, and it was more space by far than she'd ever had previously for her work. Pru positioned her easel and put up half a dozen cork boards for sketches. She wanted to capture the impression of arriving at this place, of traveling through a world of white blossoms. The image of those flowering trees filled her mind, and she was soon lost in a canvas. Tom commuted to Harrisburg five days a week, so she had ample silence and dream space for her new obsession.

Late one afternoon, Pru put down her brush and palette, wiped her hands on a rag, and stepped back to consider her progress. She was close. It was a matter now of getting the color right: the twisted branches dark, almost black, and bright patches of cerulean showing between the densely clustered flowers—shining white, delicately touched with a barely discernible vein of pink, the butter-yellow centers glowing as if a tiny nightlight had been switched on in each blossom.

Daylight declined, the sun beginning to drop into the trees that crowned the hillside to the west. There would be more light in thc cupola, and she needed to see clearly where she was before she put her work away for the day. Carefully, Pru picked up the awkward canvas by the frame. She proceeded down the hall, hesitated for a moment at the door, then pushed it open and climbed the narrow set of steps.

The wooden man sat as she'd last seen it on the day of their arrival, impassive, its back to the stairs, and Pru experienced again the eerie sense that the doll was watching the orchard, noting the flowers as they snowed down now in every breeze and littered the dust. She nodded at the figure's back. "Good afternoon, you sonofabitch." Her fear annoyed her. Trying to ignore it, Pru leaned her canvas to the right of the stairs and paused to consider it, but she was too close. She swung around, took a half-step, and froze.

The puppet had turned and now faced her. *It's looking at the painting!* The thought formed as she stumbled down the stairwell, crashing into the door. It only opened toward her, and it cost Pru a wild, panicked second to fling back the door and get through it. She rushed to her studio, found the thick yardstick that she used as a straightedge, and forced herself back to the door, cramming the piece of wood through the brass handle and across the molding.

Heart racing, she backed away.

It was dark when Tom got home. He found Pru sitting on the front steps, the door locked behind her, every light in the house blazing.

THE NEXT MORNING, over coffee, they faced each other across the kitchen table.

"You think I'm crazy, don't you?"

"No," Tom responded, "of course not. But I do think you're very imaginative, and you've been alone in this old place too much. That's my fault." Last night, he'd gone up to the widow's watch to retrieve Pru's painting and found the marionette seated as he remembered. Night had blackened the windows, turning them to mirrors, and when he's studied the carved features and his own face standing over the doll's shoulder, an eerie sense of the thing's sentience had stolen over him. His wife's story had upset Tom more than he cared to acknowledge, and he'd seen again in his mind the image of that face, blanched by lightning, staring down at him in his bed. When he climbed down the narrow stairs, he'd blocked the door to the window's watch as Pru had done.

"I want to get rid of that damn thing," she put in.

Tom nodded. "I have an idea. Let's have a yard sale." They had some heavy Victorian pieces of his grandmother's that didn't match the clean lines and simple proportions of the house and had discovered as well some leather-bound books and old coins and clothes, refuse from the lives lived there. "We'll unload all the junk that's cluttering the front parlor. It'll be fun."

"What about the marionette?"

"We'll sit his ass in a chair under the oak in the yard. Somebody will take him off our hands. I bet we could get a hundred bucks for him."

Pru brightened a little. It would be a simple matter to get the sale in the local paper, maybe put some fliers in their neighbors' mailboxes.

"Okay," she agreed. "But listen, I want that thing out of the house now. I can't stand the thought of it being in here with us."

"Fine. I'll take it out to the barn." How could he refuse such a simple request? But the thought of touching the puppet, of lifting it in his arms, filled him with dread.

She looked at him curiously. "You're scared, aren't you?"

Ten minutes later, Tom opened the barn door with his knee and carried the doll inside. The interior was murky and smelled of old leather, rat droppings, and the dusty remnants of hay. Sunbeams floated in a slant of light that angled in where planks in the wall had warped apart. Block and tackle hanging from a rafter creaked in the breeze that whisked in, and mice scurried in the far corners. Tom laid the puppet in the shadows, its back against the wall, and stepped quickly for the shape of the door outlined in light. Once the door was open, he paused and looked back, considering for a moment his childhood goblin. The arms hung limp at its sides, palms up, and the wooden head, dejected, had fallen to its chest.

He closed the door behind him and walked away.

SATURDAY CAME, and Tom and Pru were surprised at the crowd that gathered to wander among their discarded possessions. Much of the furniture, in particular, attracted attention, and they had priced things to sell. All afternoon, upwardly mobile gentry with a nose for bargains loaded walnut furniture and vintage clothes into the backs of their shining sport utility vehicles. Two couples got into a bidding war over a marble-topped end table, and Tom wound up pocketing a check for seven hundred dollars. He then turned away to find himself face to face with a prim woman, not quite elderly, who had planted herself in his path.

"Excuse me," she said. "Are you the man of the house?"

"Yes. Tom Jamieson," he replied, extending his hand.

She held out her fingers in response. "Mildred Townsend," she pronounced, a sparrow of a woman sporting a flat pill box hat from which a single blue feather curled up like a wisp of smoke. "I understand you're a McPhearson."

"On my mother's side."

"How nice," she told him, searching his face. "It's good to have the old families around. My family has lived and died in this county since before the Revolution."

It made no difference to Tom how long the remains of Mildred Townsend's ancestors had fertilized the local hillsides, but he knew enough of family history to recall that the McPhearsons had settled here after the War of 1812. The old bird was establishing a pecking order, with herself on top. Tom smiled at her with mock sweetness.

She captured his arm, and he walked her into the clutter of boxes and furniture. "Many of these things belonged to your grandmother. She was a friend of mine."

Tom recognized the implied criticism in this remark, but he said nothing. This woman was a stranger, and he had no intention of justifying himself.

"How sad she would've been to see her things out on the lawn like this!" she persisted.

His patience was wearing thin. What he really wanted to do was drop behind Mildred Townsend, step back, and plant a good swift kick on her rear end, one that would lift her a few inches from the ground and precipitate her flight. Picturing this, Tom smiled at her broadly, increasing her agitation.

They steered around a bulky armoire. A rush of breath escaped the woman, and her little claw tightened on his arm. A few feet away, Uncle Edward slumped like a corpse in his chair.

"Good Lord," she stammered. Her eyes lifted to Tom and darted back to the form sitting in the shadow of the oak. "That's Isaiah McPhearson's marionette! Sitting there—in broad daylight!"

Her hands flew to her face, and she backed away and dodged with startling agility through the browsers on the lawn. Tom saw a blue feather disappear into an old black Lincoln, and in a moment, the orchard had swallowed her car.

Good riddance, he thought, sliding his hands into the pockets of his blue jeans and rocking back on his heels. For the first time, he was grateful to the marionette.

ALL AFTERNOON, Pru had watched furtively as customers approached the wooden man. Each time, the same thing had happened. The person, man or woman, would spot the puppet and laugh. He or she would approach then to admire the fine curve of a forearm or the hinge of an elbow. At some point, however, the hand would drop from the whorl of grain on the puppet's face or torso, and the person would step away, a disquieted expression on his face. Now Pru stood on the front steps with Tom, leaning against a railing. It was six o'clock, and the browsers had all gone home with their treasures. The first intimations of the late spring twilight sifted out of the orchard, and she surveyed the yard, empty except for a single box and the mannequin sitting meditatively in its rush-bottom chair.

Pru spoke without shifting her gaze. "The whole point was to get rid of that thing."

"I was hoping to pawn it off on someone," Tom replied. "But I *do* have an alternate plan."

She looked at him doubtfully. Without speaking, he walked

off into the barn and emerged with an armful of wood. He made a pile of the smaller sticks and crossed the pile with some split pieces of planking, then returned to where Pru stood watching.

"Wood burns," he said.

Of course, she thought. *A bonfire! We'll burn the witchy thing.*

"I want to do it."

"You sure?" he asked.

"Absolutely."

Tom reached into his pocket and handed her a pack of matches. "There's a can of gasoline in the barn," he told her. "I'm gonna grab a shower. Don't burn the house down."

As soon as Pru was alone, she closed her eyes and stood silently, collecting herself. A green smell rose out of the orchard. Then she fixed her sights on the marionette sitting there so placidly, stepped up to it, and grabbed it by one wrist. She dragged it across the yard to the pile of kindling and threw it on top. The doll sprawled face down, and in her mind an uninvited vision rose up: black-and-white footage, piles and piles of bodies, horribly thin, some of them moving. She vanished into the barn, found the can of gas by the lawn mower, and walked out into the twilight.

The puppet was gone.

She dropped the can, and it sloshed at her feet.

TOM STEPPED DRIPPING out of the shower. He heard the front door slam and feet pounding up the stairs. Pru burst into the room.

"Uncle Edward's gone!"

"*What?*"

Her face was white, drained of every hint of color. "I went into the barn for the gasoline, and when I came out, he was gone."

Tom jerked on his jeans, annoyed, and pushed roughly past her. Their bedroom window looked out over the yard, and he saw the pile of kindling and a single box of books. The mannequin, as well as the chair it had sat in, had vanished.

"Someone took it," he said shortly. "Isn't that what we wanted?"

Pru leaned in the doorway, holding herself in her arms, her eyes huge. "Everyone went home, Tom. There's no one here but us."

"Oh, come on!" he scoffed. He meant to halt her train of thought before it ran away with her.

A chair scraped above their heads. Tom leaned past her, and in unison, they looked down the hall and saw that the door to widow's watch stood open.

"Oh, my God! *My God!*" Pru flattened herself against the wall as if she meant to merge with it and disappear.

"Stay here."

Tom moved down the hall, eyes fixed on the open doorway. The stairs were nearly vertical, and he climbed them like a ladder, a boy again, not making a sound. When he reached the top, he paused before looking: the marionette sat in its chair as usual, its back to the stairs. No one else was there.

Backing down, he felt as if he were sinking through dark water. At the bottom of the well, he found his wife staring at him.

"It's up there, isn't it?" Her voice cracked.

He nodded. Pru's words seemed to reach him from an impossible distance.

All at once, her hand reached for the yardstick leaning by the door and thrust it through the handle. He heard her steps descending rapidly to the first floor and descending again, growing fainter, and in a minute she was back, swinging wildly at the door with a hammer. After a moment, Tom understood what she was trying to do.

"Let me," he said.

At first, Pru merely glared at him defiantly, but then, seeing that he meant to help, she relented. Tom took the wooden-handled hammer from her shaking hand and pried the rusted sixteen-penny nails from her clenched fist.

He positioned a nail at the edge of the molding, tapped it into place, and then drove it savagely through the molding and into the door. He didn't stop until a dozen nails sealed that door.

IV

NEITHER OF THEM could say with any final assurance why they remained in the house. In part, it was a refusal to be driven away; if one admits a fear, one has to live afraid. Tom accepted this theory—and in fact, he convinced himself that someone had dragged the puppet upstairs intentionally to frighten them (perhaps that horrid Townsend woman)—but Pru realized, she *knew*, that there was another possibility entirely. How could they walk away from something, however dark, that so enlarged the boundaries of their world? So Tom went to work and Pru painted in her back room, and neither of them mentioned the door nailed shut down the hall, though they thought of little else. Old houses creak and sigh, and sometimes, hearing this, Pru would look from her canvas and imagine the mannequin pacing the confines of its chamber, gaining power like a genie trapped in a bottle, while the green fruit grew round in the orchard. Spring passed, the days lengthening into June and gradually becoming shorter again, until it was late September. The nights were cold now, and the stars seemed whiter, closer. All night, apples hung in the air that smelled like ice—little mirrors, flecks of light like the swirl of constellations on their deepening skins.

It was four in the morning, the blank, still time before dawn, empty of movement and sound. Tom was dreaming. Isaiah McPhearson slashed one-armed with an axe at the trunk of an apple tree, his black hair flying. Fruit thumped to the ground, knocking, pattering like the first big drops before a deluge, and then the rain needled down. The yellow stripe on Isaiah's uniform pants crackled like a flash of lightning, and the tree crashed to the earth.

Tom sat upright, instantly awake. Had he heard something? All was silent now, only the rush of blood in his ears. A faint creak sounded, and after three long seconds, another one: someone was coming up the stairs, slowly, as silently as possible. He sensed this more than hearing it, as if the blackness around him was stirred by motion. Soft steps reached the top of the stairs and turned left into his study, the room on the other side of the wall behind the headboard. Pru slept soundly beside him, oblivious, wrapped in the blankets. He decided not to wake her; after all, he might be imagining things. Tom reached for the Louisville Slugger leaning by the bed, a boy's bat he'd purchased one day on his lunch hour. It was small enough to swing and maneuver easily in one hand, but thick enough, he knew, to break bones. The salesman had assumed he was buying it for his son, and Tom had seen no reason to disabuse the man. The incident that spring with the puppet had unnerved him more than he liked to admit; and the idea that a neighbor, someone who knew the history of his family, had secretly carried the doll inside to terrify them bothered him almost as much as the alternative.

Deliberately, he closed his fingers around the grip, swung his legs to the floor, and moved stealthily into the hall—pausing a few feet from the study door, listening, listening, the bat poised in his hand. The moon had gone down hours ago, and peering into the blackened doorway was like staring into a cave. From inside, Tom heard a sound, faint but unmistakable: a scraping, a drawer being opened. His mind showed him a picture of the marionette standing at his desk, and the horror, the cold dread he felt at this vision, was more than he could tolerate—he *had* to know, to face it. In one motion, he entered, flicked on the switch at the wall, and stepped to the middle of the room.

No one stood at the desk. Relief washed over him, and he lowered the bat; but then his mind registered movement over his shoulder. Tom told himself to turn, to raise the bat to block the descending blow, but it was too late. A sharp pain in his neck filled his brain with an explosion of light, and his legs wouldn't hold him. He wasn't sure how much time passed, but then he saw an arm lying on the floor and realized it was *his* and knew his bloody head rested on that arm. At the same moment, he was dimly aware of footsteps moving down the hall.

Pru, he thought.

He heard her stir awake behind the wall, and the bed creaked. "*What?*" He heard the grogginess in her voice, then the panic. "*Who are you?*" she screamed, and Tom struggled to his knees, steadying himself on a corner of the desk, his head spinning, ready to burst. Pru screamed again, and something thumped sickeningly against the wall. He looked toward the door, trying to get up, to reach it, and heard a loud cracking noise he could not identify. Then a figure moved quickly past the door toward the bedroom. *Two of them!* he thought. This time he forced himself to his feet, but his knees buckled, and he dropped face down with a groan. Next door, the bed scraped, flesh slammed against flesh, and something fell heavily to the floor. Footsteps approached down the hall and paused, and Tom raised his head to see.

The puppet stood in the doorway, gazing down at him.

The look they exchanged could not have lasted long as the clock measures time, but it contained a weight of recognition, and the years that had passed since he was six compressed to an instant. Then something clattered to the floor, and the mannequin turned away. Tom heard it creak up the stairs to the cupola. His eyes focused on a hunting knife lying inches from his face, its serrated blade smeared with gore.

Sliding unsteadily along the wall, Tom made his way to the bedroom and turned on a lamp. Pru crouched in a corner, nearly catatonic with shock. He went to her, and when he was certain that she wasn't hurt, he followed her eyes to the form lying on the floor. Disoriented, Tom thought at first that the man had nothing but deep, spreading shadow where his head should've been. Then he realized that the intruder wore a black stocking pulled down over his face. Moving closer, he saw that the man's throat had been slashed: the shadow was blood.

The dead man's eyes stared at the ceiling.

Tom called the police from his study. He had the foresight to pick up the knife and grip the handle before dropping it to the floor. Returning to the bedroom, he attempted to coax Pru from her corner, but she shook her head, adamant, childish in her refusal, and he understood that to move her then would break her. He put his arms around her, and they clung there together. It was nearly dawn. In a few minutes, he heard tires screeching up in the yard below, and blue lights circled the walls.

V

THE FOLLOWING THREE DAYS were a blur of nurses, detectives, and reporters. Pru's left shoulder had been dislocated when the intruder had thrown her against the wall, and Tom had a concussion, but they were otherwise unharmed. The police kept telling them how lucky they were, and only the two of them realized how true that was. Tom handled all the questions from reporters while Pru sat silent, holding his hand, and he kept their story straight. The man had broken a window to get in, and he had a long history of violence and drug abuse. The police found Tom's prints on the man's knife, and it all seemed simple enough: Tom was a hero. They endured seeing their faces on the evening news and waited for their fifteen minutes of fame to end and for the world to forget about them.

But it was far from simple. Both of them had trouble sleeping, but it was not from fear, not exactly; they knew they couldn't possibly be safer in that house.

One blue afternoon in October, Tom and Pru wandered together in the orchard. High up, flocks of blackbirds scrawled their disappearance across the sky, a script Pru felt she could decipher. Apples hung red and heavy on the trees, and she reached up, plucked one, and polished it against her crimson sweater. The apple was sweet and tart at once, tasting of the season, of the last warm sunlight, cold stones, and fallen leaves.

She handed Tom the red fruit with a white gash in the shape of her mouth. "Taste this."

The apple cracked when he bit into it, and Pru watched her husband chewing thoughtfully, looking over the treetops toward the house. The cupola seemed to float in the blue air, suspended, unattached to any earthly anchoring, the outline of the mannequin barely visible behind the flashing glass.

"What are we going to do?" she asked him.

Tom's eyes never left the cupola. "We can't walk away," he responded at last. "And we can't just pretend this didn't happen. We need to make a place for this thing in our lives."

Pru nodded slowly, considering. She thought so, too. They felt rooted to the place now, linked to the silent presence that sat unmoving in the glass room at the top of their house.

So Tom pulled the nails out of the molding, filled the holes with wood putty, and painted. They cleaned the glass in the widow's watch inside and out and hung pots of ivy and arrowhead fern from the ceiling. Pru clipped a shoot in the orchard, rooted it in a jar of water, and placed the potted apple tree at the marionette's feet. Once a week, summer and winter, they climbed the stairs together to dust and water the plants. At night, the creaks and groans they heard moving down the hallways or filling with a single note the dark immensity of distant rooms could've been the old house settling into the earth. They slept more soundly when they locked the bedroom door, though they both knew that wooden fingers could turn a key as well as any.

Pru became pregnant, and one afternoon when she was nearly ready to deliver the child, as she and Tom performed their weekly ritual in the cupola, she thought the puppet turned, infinitesimally, to observe her. With the exception of that one uncertain instance, neither of them ever again saw the doll move.

A son was born to the Jamiesons, and they named him Isaiah. On rainy Saturday afternoons, the boy crept just far enough up the narrow stairs to the cupola to peek, mesmerized, at his birthright, the wooden man his parents refused to discuss.

Endlessly patient, Uncle Edward sat in his arboretum. In the house below, those others talked and cried and made love, made the heat rise like breath in the rooms, a presence always on the periphery. From the grainy whorl of his eyes, he stared out into the rolling landscape: a crow and its shadow sliding over the snow, the first blur of spring a mist over everything, then blossoms turning to fruit, the orchard and distant hills red and yellow and ocher with the slow burn of autumn—all of this passing like pictures in a gallery. The marionette, enchanted by the changing earth from which he'd sprung, called out in his silent manner to his sources.

The Blue Garden

Not wanting to be stopped or asked where he was going in such a hurry, the boy glided quickly to the border of the yard, stepping up carefully into his father's rock garden—the first level, then the second, his nose registering the sharp, musky scent of tomato vines. Sometimes at dusk deer would come to stand at the edge of the garden, perfectly still, listening with their entire bodies. If he looked away for an instant, they'd be gone, leaving only the crescent shapes of their hoof-prints pressed into the dirt for him to find in the morning. The boy tried now to be like those deer, to disappear as they did, silently, without moving.

So he vanished into the trees. The leaves, far above his head, spread out to block the sun, and he breathed in the smell of cool stone and green shadow and earth. Birds flitted noiselessly from trunk to rough gray trunk as he wove through the woods, until the trees opened and spilled him into the light.

A scattering of white, rain-eaten headstones surrounded a single dark cedar, the pieces of a broken marble cross at its base. The land sloped down from Springfield Avenue and the muted rush of traffic, the white spire of the Presbyterian Church rising above the tree-line in the distance. When Washington retreated south from New York in 1776, he stopped here to bury his dead.

Fifty years later, the town put in headstones, and now the English-sounding names on those stones—*Nathaniel Proctor, Samuel Cuthbert*—had been nearly erased by the weather. At the end of May, men came in a long black car and placed a flag with a circle of thirteen stars on each grave; but the summer was nearly over now, and the little flags fluttering in the breeze had turned to tattered patches of pink and blue rag clinging to a stick. The boy pulled a flag like a flower from the grave at his feet and counted the stars.

A friend at school told him he'd seen a strange man standing at the foot of a grave one night—at a tipped stone in the back corner where the hedge threw shadow. The man's back had been turned, his long hair tied in a ponytail. The boy didn't believe his friend, but he avoided the place after dark just the same. He stepped softly now, listening to the wind move in the long grass, and imagined the soldiers sleeping under his feet in their slowly fading blue coats.

The boy had visited the graveyard many times before, had even climbed the old cedar and looked down at the headstones like a row of crooked teeth. But today he found the place where the barbed wire running along the hedge bordering the cemetery to the east had rusted through, and he stepped carefully past the wire, trying not to snag his tee shirt or jeans, and pushed his way through the black hedge.

To his surprise, he emerged in a garden. The back of a crooked gray house with gables overlooked a yard that sloped downhill to the woods. A thin strip of grass ran down the middle of the yard from the house to the trees, and on both sides of this path, filling the rest of the space, were bright beds of irises. The flowers rose higher than his head, wavering slightly in the breeze, a dense, blue fire of irises. The butterflies that hovered over the flowers here were not the pale, butter-colored scraps of life the size of his thumb-top that he'd seen drifting over his father's garden, but huge, gaudy things bigger than his fist: tiger swallowtails, southern belles, a pair of orange monarchs with their black-veined wings like stained glass.

Entranced, the boy wandered down the path, gazing up at the blue, loose-mouthed irises. They seemed to lean over him, bending down in the breeze to whisper, their lisp so thick the words came out as soft, sibilant *s*'s, the sound of blood rushing in his ears.

There was no sign of life at the house. Still, he imagined an old woman watching from behind the lace curtains, her eyes magnified behind the lenses of her glasses, a woman who was strange and far away like his father's mother. Earlier that summer, he and his older brother and his father had gone to move her out of her house. In the dark third floor attic smelling of dust and mildew, they'd come upon the accumulated junk of eighty years or more—broad-brimmed lady's hats with silk flowers or dyed feathers, cracked high-button shoes that would never be worn again, a dusty black derby. The boy found a parasol, and when he opened it, the rotted silk fell away, leaving him standing like Robinson Crusoe with the open frame in his hand, the absent parasol raised against an imagined sun. Reaching with two fingers into the inside pocket of a black suit coat, he drew out a ten-dollar bill, Confederate, frail and worn as onionskin; it had an old brown bloodstain on it, and the boy slipped the bill furtively into his pocket. He later took the derby to school for show-and-tell, but the blood-stained Confederate money he pressed in the pages of a book, a secret he showed to no one.

That day, the boy and his older brother had thrown from the narrow attic window old clothes that mimicked the shape of people as they dropped to the yard below. A few rags had caught to hang in the apple tree. His father gathered the wreckage into a pile, and every now and then, the old woman, his grandmother, would burst from the back door to snatch some fragment of herself from the lawn and disappear back inside, clutching her treasure to her breast. The boy remembered the bonfire they'd made, the scraps of burning silk and wool lifting in the wind, the glowing ashes. Three weeks later, his grandmother was dead. Now, as he walked past the tall rows of irises, he thought, *We should've planted flowers*. Better the cool blue flames of these irises, the kaleidoscope of butterflies shifting over them, than the hot smell of that bonfire, the drifting ashes, the old woman screaming at them from her kitchen window . . .

A loud *bang* from the house behind him startled the boy—someone had slammed a door in the silence, and he felt the hair rise in a cold path across his scalp. He sensed the eyes of the old woman in the house boring into him, hostile and unforgiving, and he knew he was guilty for burning his grandmother's things. He imagined, on the other side of the hedge, the ragged blue soldiers pulling themselves up from their graves and stumbling toward him, their hands lifted accusingly.

In a sudden panic, he sprinted for the woods. He dashed through the trees and slammed full-speed into a thicket of blackberries, turning helplessly and emerging, at last, into a world he recognized: the sunlight slanting across a neighbor's backyard.

The boy fell gratefully to his knees, panting for air, his face and hands torn from the brambles, his clothes stained from the dark fruit.

YEARS LATER, the boy, nearly an old man now, was wandering in a junk shop in the city where he lived, a thousand miles from the town where he'd grown up. He stepped past a row of armoires, running his hand briefly over the sturdy chests, the polished swirl of oak or black walnut, and paused before the last one. The door was ajar, and when he swung it open, he found an old black derby on the shelf inside. He took the thing into his hands: there was dust in the brim, and the leather sweatband was cracked and crumbling away. The man couldn't name what the hat reminded him of; he didn't know why he wanted it, since the moth-eaten old relic was worth nothing by the usual measure of such things. The woman at the counter glanced up from her book and watched him over the top of her glasses as he approached.

"How much for the chapeau?" he inquired, the derby hooked on his index finger.

"That thing?" she smiled doubtfully, rolling her eyes at the ceiling. "I'll let you have it for ten bucks."

So he bought the derby and took it home, where he placed it on his kitchen table.

That evening, the man kept muting the noise of the television and walking away to lean in the doorway of his shadowy kitchen, gazing at the derby, wondering. A vague smell of smoke curled from the brim, as if someone had worn it long ago to dance at a bonfire. He felt there was something forming in the dark cavity under the hat, something mysterious, something terrible and wonderful at once, but he wouldn't lift it, afraid that he'd find the table empty and the strange spell broken. He dreamed that night about irises growing on a grave in the moonlight, the name on the white headstone nearly erased by the weather.

And for days afterward, he carried that picture in his mind. The words he used to conjure what he'd seen—*loose mouths, blue flesh, moonlight*—translated him somehow out of himself, so he went through the day with his mind in another world, thinking.

The Tea Roses

I

When Travis Karlson arrived on Galveston Island on July 18, the charcoal from the previous weekend's cookouts was just beginning to crumble to dust in the backyard grills of the East End. I didn't set eyes on him until a few days later, but Hannah, standing at her window that morning with a cup of coffee steaming in her hand, spotted him almost immediately. A man in his forties, she guessed, who looked as if ash had been blown into his brown hair, wearing a pair of faded jeans and a much-washed short-sleeved shirt that had once been red.

The stranger stood riveted in front of the abandoned house next to Hannah's shotgun bungalow, the second-story porch looming over him. Something in the man's manner, some strained level of attention, attracted Hannah's notice and made her instantly curious. He lingered at the curb, staring up at the weather-beaten, unpainted house as the morning light, filtered through the twisted branches of a hundred-year-old live oak, flowed over him.

"Tourist," Hannah muttered to herself, but something told her he wasn't.

People came from all over the South and Midwest to walk the

streets of the East End Historical District in the summer. They were easy to spot, tripping over the uneven, root-lifted sidewalks as they gawked at the old houses trimmed with gingerbread. Like most of us, Hannah Winder had grown accustomed to the lush, tumbledown feel of the East End. Live oaks formed tunnels over the streets, broods of doves cooed incessantly from branches draped with Spanish moss, and bells tolling from white steeples floated in the sea breeze over rows of crooked houses from another century. All of this was familiar and comforting to Hannah. She was no longer awed: it was home.

She walked to the kitchen to warm her coffee, passing the sound of a television playing in a room off the hall. Ruby's dark eyes were glued to the set, watching an old Road Runner cartoon Hannah remembered from when she was a little girl. When she returned, the man was still rooted at the curb, apparently lost in thought as he stared up at the house. *What on earth is he so interested in?* Hannah wondered. The place next door was a two-story Queen Anne with a porch on each floor, a corner turret that lifted into the tangle of branches; but there were many such houses in the neighborhood, most of them in better repair. The wrought-iron fence with its rusted spires could barely contain the overgrown hedges of oleander framing the shallow front yard. Morning light filtered through the trees, submerging the house in green shadow that washed like a tide over hand-blown glass and carved wood.

As Hannah watched, the man strode suddenly through the gate and up the front steps to the threshold. To her surprise, he fit a key into the salt-stained lock and stepped across the encaustic tile entrance into the house. Then she noticed the Land Rover, crammed with suitcases and boxes, parked at the curb.

"Well, I'll be damned."

She wandered down the hall and poked her head into the television room.

"Hey, Honey, guess what?"

Ruby turned her pale, expressionless face to her mother.

"It looks like we're going to have a new neighbor next door. Won't that be nice?"

Silently, the child returned her gaze to the television. Ruby's dark auburn hair, falling halfway down her back, accentuated the pallor of her complexion. Hannah observed her daughter for a moment, a recurrent sadness leaking into her face, then proceeded down the hall to the kitchen.

She sat at the table nursing her second cup of coffee, leafing absent-mindedly through the newspaper to delay getting ready for work, when she saw the newcomer emerge suddenly, noisily, on his second-story veranda. He had banged through the French doors to lean over the railing, staring down the street past the front of her house, his grip white-knuckled on the banister. The man strained so far forward that Hannah was afraid he'd lose his balance and tumble head-first to the weedy front lawn. His expression suggested that he was looking for something he didn't want to find.

Curious, she stepped down the hall to a front window and looked out at the street. Behind the trunk of a live oak, out of sight of her neighbor's veranda, stood an old man in a gray sweater vest, the brim of his fedora pulled low over his face. For some reason, Hannah's eyes lingered on him. There was a stillness about him, a vaguely unnerving sense of isolation. Feeling himself observed, the old man lifted his gaze to Hannah and scowled. His eyes were cold and gray, the color of dirty ice behind the lenses of his wireframe glasses.

Shaking off her uneasiness, Hannah frowned back at him and headed for the shower. When she passed the side window, she saw that her neighbor had disappeared inside.

HANNAH TOLD ME the next day about the newcomer. On her

way home from work, she stopped at a house I was working on to fill me in. We had recently broken up, at her insistence, and were in that awkward phase of trying to figure out if we could be friends. That afternoon, I got my first taste of the ache and frustration I would suffer from for the rest of that summer: her interest in another man.

"Nick," she began, clearly excited, "somebody's moved in next door!"

He could be just house hunting, she said, but something in the way he looked up at the place, some recognition and purpose in his demeanor, not to mention the key in his pocket and the lack of a realtor's ugly white lock-box on the gate, told her he meant to live there. She smiled, tossing her light brown hair back over one shoulder—it would be good to see some life next door. The house had been empty the entire time she'd lived next to it, and she'd often worried about Ruby playing around the rickety structure or in its overgrown yard. Empty houses sometimes attracted vagrants, and one tottering old place on Church Street had become infested with scores of feral cats. She spoke quickly, breathlessly. It would be safer for Ruby, she said, if the man had come to stay.

Listening, I kept a carefully blank smile on my face. I decided to meet this guy and take his measure as soon as possible.

Hannah spent a lot of time worrying about her little girl. Ruby had loved her gruff, hard-handed father, and his absence from her life was an enigma she couldn't grasp. She'd rejected every attempt on her mother's part to explain that he was dead. One night when we were still an item, Hannah woke and heard footsteps moving through the house. Alarmed, she shook me awake, and we got up to find Ruby's bed empty. We found her in the parlor, staring intently out the window. When asked what she was doing, the child turned to her mother a stubborn, disquieting face.

I knew: she was looking for her father.

Jon Winder had been a commercial fisherman, and it seemed with each passing season he needed to go farther out to sea for the good runs of snapper or yellowtail. Money had been scarce for the previous year or more, so Winder and his crew had gone out for a last run before some bad weather that was approaching from the southeast. Somehow, the storm had caught them, even though they knew it was coming. They must've had engine trouble, but Hannah would never know for sure. No trace of the boat was ever found. She felt it was her fault that Jon was dead. He would never have taken the risk, she said, if not for her constant worries and complaints about money.

After Jon's death, Hannah closed up the house and took Ruby to her parents' farm in Missouri along the Mississippi River, her girlhood home. She enrolled her daughter in a local preschool and eased gratefully into the familiar pattern of the farm, a sense of time based more on seasons than on clocks. Hannah saw the things of the earth, apparently so frail and evanescent, persisting with a stubborn hardihood. Everything, in its time, returned; everything came back. Perhaps her life would bloom again, as well.

That spring, the March rains washed away the last rags of snow, an expected, yearly cleansing; but the rain continued to fall for weeks, and the river, already swollen with winter runoff, began to rise. Each night on the news, they watched the steady, inexorable approach of the flood from the north, her father's face etched with concern. The Mississippi and its tributaries overflowed their banks again and again, covering fields of corn and spring wheat and, in some cases, entire towns with seven feet or more of silt- and debris-laden water. Hannah worked furiously for three days, stacking sandbags with her neighbors and a squad from the Army Corps of Engineers as rain ticked at her yellow slicker, a strand of water-darkened hair plastered to one cheek. They were building a wall to hold back disaster.

On a shelf of her bedroom closet, she discovered a stack of

books from high school, including a copy of *The Great Gatsby*. At sixteen, she'd found the novel ponderous and irrelevant, but now Fitzgerald's lyric evocation of lost love and obsession spoke eloquently to her. She read a few chapters a night, falling then into exhausted sleep and dreams of rising water. On the third day, the rain fell hard and steady, and it seemed the whole world was about to be submerged. A line from the end of *Gatsby* replayed in her mind as she lifted and handed on the heavy bags of sand: *Blessed are the dead that the rain falls on*.

Their levee saved the town, but fields were swallowed and crops ruined. Her father was lucky; he only lost about fifteen acres of corn, low land that ran directly along the river. The half-submerged corn rose like reeds from the muddy water, the green field of her childhood transformed into a delta. After a few days, the water fell away, leaving pools, rotted stalks, and a slick, muddy expanse loud with flies and brain-shaped clouds of gnats.

One evening at sunset, Hannah walked at the edge of the field of oats that covered the bluff overlooking the drowned field. The vermilion disk of sun touched the hills to the west, turning the water red. Suddenly, her eye was drawn to movement in the field below—a figure rose and stood, knee-deep in mud. A man, sixty or seventy feet beneath her.

He was terribly thin, with lank hair falling past his shoulders. Silhouetted against the dusk-reddened river, his form was draped in a long coat, and his fingers, dripping with mud, extended from one ragged sleeve. Lifting his knees, he struggled to free himself, and as Hannah watched, other figures rose from the darkening slime behind him. One had a cap, brimmed, the kind worn by cadets at military academies, and a rope of dirty gold braid on his sleeve glowed in the last daylight. A woman stood waist-deep behind him, her long dark hair swamp-slicked, wearing what looked like a muslin dress. Six forms in all—some nearly shapeless, obscured and struggling in the mud, trapped like flies on fly-paper.

A gasp escaped Hannah, and it carried in the sundown stillness. With one gesture, the six dark heads turned and looked up.

Who were they? It was too murky to see their faces, but she was certain they saw her, fixed her with gazes that felt predatory and full of longing. Hannah's isolation and vulnerability washed over her. They began to struggle toward her through the mud, a seventh and eighth figure rising as they came.

Rigid with dread, Hannah was unable to take her eyes away from their slow approach; she felt their dumb need pulling at her, touching her with invisible fingers. *Intolerable*: the word floated up in her mind. What she witnessed, what would happen if she did not run, soon, was more than she could bear. She wrestled with a cold, white fear that robbed her of the ability to think or move. Her legs felt like water, threatening to collapse and spill her to the earth, to roll her downhill toward *them*.

The gaunt, shapeless figures slogged toward her, the leader in his greatcoat only a few feet now from the base of the solid rise on which Hannah stood.

Intolerable.

At last her legs obeyed, and she raced through the oats, heart pounding, in a two-mile dash for the house. Hannah dreaded fainting before she reached safety, imagining those awful figures following her trail of crushed stalks through the field, stumbling upon her in the dark.

What if she lost her direction in the shifting maze of oats and couldn't find her way home? She didn't dare look behind her. Finally, she glimpsed a lighted bedroom window rising above the grain. Hannah stumbled up the back steps and burst into the kitchen, hysterical and insect-bitten, oat-chaff tangled in her long brown hair, and found her mother calmly washing dishes at the sink. She could never convey to either of her parents a word of what had happened.

The next morning, her father made a gruesome discovery. Eight desiccated corpses, some of them in uniforms, lay face-down in his ruined cornfield. The pattern in the mud, as he informed Hannah and her mother that evening, looked like the bodies had crawled or waded before collapsing; but that was impossible, of course—the trails must have been made by withdrawing water. Her father called the police. The coroner took the bodies away and searched unsuccessfully for others, and after a few days, the rest of the story fell into place. An old graveyard upstream in Illinois, dating back to the Civil War, had been overrun by the flood, and rotted coffins drifted up in the watery earth and broke open. Corpses floated downstream, some of them traveling hundreds of miles in the swift currents to arrive in a Missouri cornfield.

Her father joked that the South had been invaded again, and by the same damned army as last time.

Blessed are the dead that the rain falls on.

Not long after, Hannah left her parents' farm. She returned to Galveston, where she owned her bungalow in the East End. Jon had seen to that. She and Ruby went back to their island of flowering oleander and old tea roses, to tunnels of live oaks and murmuring doves. Hannah had been happy there, and perhaps she could be again, even without Jon. It was the only place where Ruby had known her father. Soon, Hannah convinced herself that her experience above the flooded Missouri cornfield had been a dream, or some sort of hallucination brought on by weeks of work and continual rain. She understood that stress and exhaustion can magnify the power of suggestion. *The brain is wider than the sky*, as a poem in another of her high school texts had put it. What had happened didn't fit with any picture of the world she could accept. She'd seen something that simply was not there.

Hannah was only thirty-two, but she felt she had already lived one life. Back on the island, she wanted to begin a new one. She landed a job as a secretary at the local State Farm office, hoping to make a decent home for Ruby. She wanted to get away from the past, to escape her dead, but it seemed that her little girl called out to it incessantly.

I FIRST MET HANNAH on the breezy back patio of a Mexican restaurant at Tenth and Market, my usual hangout at the time. The food there was inexpensive and good, and the Carta Blancas were always ice cold. I suppose, in some ways, I was an easy man to please. Until Hannah Winder came into my life, there had never been anything I wanted badly that I couldn't find a way to get. I had no ambitions, and thus no disappointments. But then I saw Hannah sitting at a candle-lit table across the patio, the sea breeze lifting her long, caramel-colored hair, her white-faced little girl like a mortuary statue at her side.

I was recently back on the island myself. When I completed my undergraduate work at UT, I hung around Austin for a few years more and picked up an M.A., mainly because of some professors I liked and the great blues and rockabilly you could hear then in the bars on Sixth Street. I was born and raised in Galveston, though, the youngest of six sons of Greek parents. The man I was named after, my great-great grandfather Nicholas Papanopoulis, had arrived on the island from Athens in 1898. When the ethnocentric, fourth-generation Scotch-English immigration agents couldn't pronounce his name, they changed it to Pauley, and there have been Pauleys in Galveston ever since. So, with no definite plans, I guess it was natural that my life would wash back up onto Galveston's muddy beaches. I restored a broken-down Eastlake cottage on Market Street and settled in.

Since the hurricane that swallowed the city in 1900, bringing the town's economic glory days to a sudden end, money has never been plentiful on the island. I taught part-time at the community college. Bone-head English, mainly—you know, trying to show under-prepared freshman who had no business being in college how to get their subjects and verbs to agree. Every now and then, the dean would let me do a literature class—just to keep me hooked, I think—so occasionally I had the opportunity to indulge my interest in American writing. I like to imagine that if Faulkner had ever spent any time on the island, if he had gotten a good look at those salt-eaten Victorian houses with their gardens of overgrown tea roses and heard the story of the 1900 hurricane, he would've set a novel there, or at least a damn good short story. How could he possibly have resisted all that tragedy and decay? In Galveston, the past was an active force, visible everywhere you looked.

I didn't make much money teaching; nobody ever does. So I began to supplement my income by doing restorations. People saw what I'd done with my bungalow, and word got around.

Also, I sold a little marijuana on the side. To survive in Galveston, you had to become a bit of an entrepreneur. When I came back to the island after Austin, I brought an ounce of weed with me, high-grade stuff from Northern California. I put aside the seeds from my bag, laying them for a few days in some paper towels I kept damp. The ones that germinated, I planted; then I fixed up a closet in the back of my bungalow with sun-lamps and foil on the walls and ceiling to reflect the light. I kept a dozen good-sized plants in there. A few times a year, when the crop flowered, I harvested; a little for my personal use, and the rest I sold. Never in quantity, just a lid here and there to house clients mostly, upstanding citizens in their sixties who had fond memories of the Summer of Love. People like that, I reasoned, would never go to the seedy parts of town for weed, so the bad boys, the ones who sold the stuff in quantity and made enormous profits, never knew I was skimming from their business. My clients smoked privately in their dens and bedrooms, so the chances that they'd get busted and expose me were slim to none. Dealing strictly with them, I could fly low, under police radar; but I needed to keep my business small and select.

When my relatives found out about my illicit sideline, most of them refused to talk to me. I became the black sheep, the one the family matriarchs pointed out as an object lesson to various cousins and nephews. With my long black hair and earring, the Grateful Dead skull-and-roses tattoo I sported on my left shoulder, I must've looked the part, but I figured they'd forgive me eventually. After all, blood is thicker than water, especially for Greeks.

So there I was, a year past thirty, halfway through my second cold beer of the evening, when Hannah sat down, helping her silent little girl into the chair beside her. I saw right away how beautiful Hannah Winder was. She noticed me looking at her, and a little grin curled the edge of her mouth.

I got up, walked over, and introduced myself.

"Are you a pirate?" Ruby asked, regarding me with her frank brown eyes.

"Sweetheart, don't be rude," Hannah cut in, but she couldn't repress a chuckle at my expense.

"Not at the moment," I answered the little girl, and then shifted my eyes to her mother.

"But I'd be willing to try anything if I thought there was a buck in it."

Hannah laughed, and it seemed to add a glow to her face in the candlelight. Her right hand rested on the stem of her wine glass, the ring finger bare. I saw my chance and pushed ahead before I lost my nerve.

"I don't mean to intrude," I began, "but I'd really like to take you out some time."

People at nearby tables stopped talking so they could listen. Hannah's dark brown eyes, nearly black in the half-light, fell on me with a weight I could feel in my gut.

"That would be nice," she smiled.

A few moments later I stepped away, her phone number on a cocktail napkin tucked securely in the pocket of my denim shirt. I felt like I'd just won the Texas Lotto.

We were happy for a while, but that was the end of my period of ease and contentment. By the time Travis set foot on the island, Hannah had decided that a carpenter and part-time drug dealer with vague literary aspirations was not the kind of man her troubled daughter needed as a father. So my bad luck, my heartache, became Travis's opportunity.

II

GRADUALLY, NOT WISHING to appear too inquisitive, Travis's neighbors began to stroll across the street, bringing casseroles or cakes, as Southerners will. Travis would offer them a glass of iced tea and sit on the steps for twenty minutes, smiling enigmatically as they gently probed him for information. His name was Travis Karlson. He was an architect. Divorced. He planned to restore the house completely and sell it. This last piece of information always pleased them, since any reclaimed property would raise the value of their homes as well. Travis politely turned down invitations to church picnics or softball games, claiming he had too much work to do.

Then his visitor—a lone husband or a couple sometimes—would rise, shake his hand, and bid him welcome, leaving an empty glass on the front steps, a soaked wedge of lemon in the bottom.

It was around this same time, in late July as the full force of the summer heat slammed down on the island, that I first came to see him, too; ostensibly, to offer my services as a carpenter and all-round house repairman, but more truly to check out the man who, in my opinion, found himself in much too close a proximity to Hannah Winder.

One evening after work, I discovered him kneeling at the side of the house, back turned, tapping down the lid of a paint can with a hammer, his aluminum ladder folded up and lying in the grass. I'd come silently around the corner, and I must've startled him. He turned, his grip tightening instinctively on the hammer, but he relaxed as soon as his eyes took me in.

"Can I help you?"

"Sorry," I said. "Didn't mean to disturb you. I just wanted to drop by and introduce myself. I'm Nick Pauley. I do house repairs. Restorations. I've worked on a number of places on this block."

He stood, and I had a good chance to appraise him. He was my height, maybe an inch or so shorter. At first, I thought he'd gotten paint in his hair, but then I realized he was going gray. That surprised me: he was lean and tan from working outside, his tee shirt and faded jeans lightly speckled with pale yellow paint, and I couldn't figure out if he was older than he looked or younger and turning gray early.

He stepped forward and thrust out his hand. I took it automatically, then made it a point to return the pressure. "Travis Karlson. You're not disturbing me. I was just packing it in." Searching my face for a moment, he asked, "Want a beer?"

That, I admit, surprised me. I already knew that everyone else got iced tea.

"Sure," I smiled, deciding to go with it. A cold beer sounded damn good. Besides, it would give me a chance to check him out more thoroughly, maybe ask a few questions. He seemed pleased that I'd accepted.

"C'mon in," he said, walking past me to the front of the house. He'd almost finished putting a coat of yellow paint on the place. The battered shutters, already primed, had been removed from the windows and leaned against the base of the porch, waiting for a new coat of enamel to bring them back to life. I followed him up the steps. "You live around here, Nick?" he asked over his shoulder.

"A few blocks away, on Market." By this time, we were through the storm doors and the front door with its beveled glass oval. That was the first time I'd been in that house. The shadows loomed thick and dusty, as if they had substance; the air was dank. I glanced down the hall, a little ill at ease. A few paces in front of me, a staircase rose to the second floor. Doors to the right and left opened into rooms I couldn't see.

Travis was watching me, though he took pains to conceal it.

"So, you've worked on some places around here?"

"I've done two restorations on this block alone," I said, going into my sales pitch. "That Queen Anne down the street . . ."

"Ever see anything odd?" he interrupted me.

I took a second to try to read his face. "Odd how?"

He shrugged and turned away, stepping into the front parlor. Crossing the vacant room, he laid a palm on the half-open pocket door between the parlor and what appeared to be a dining room. Behind him, I caught a glimpse of a chandelier draped in cobwebs.

"Can you believe that someone painted over this?" he asked, sliding his eyes toward me.

The door rolled easily on its casters, nearly reaching the nine-foot ceiling. "Who in the world would do such a thing?"

It took a moment to realize he was waiting for a response.

"People lived in these places for years," I managed, "before anyone had any sense of their historical value. You wouldn't believe what I find in some of them."

Those old houses, the ones that had survived the hurricane, were full of exotic woods. After the Civil War, Galveston had been the busiest port in the country outside of New York, and ships from all over the world docked along Avenue A on the bay side of the island and unloaded the timber they'd carried for ballast. It was cheaper and easier back then to go down to the docks and pick up someone's cast off teak, mahogany, or cypress than it was to pay for American pine or white oak.

"I want to take this thing down," he said, his hand still on the pocket door, "sand off the paint, and stain it. Find out what's underneath. But I'll need some help. The door's too heavy for one man."

"Just let me know when," I told him.

Again it struck me: the man was watching me, waiting for something. Then I realized: *he doesn't like this place either*—it felt wrong to him—and he was weighing me, trying to gauge my reaction. My poor attempt to be business-like hadn't fazed him at all.

"Let's go out back," he suggested. "There's no place to get comfortable inside."

So he led me through the dining room and adjoining kitchen to his back steps, stopping at the refrigerator for two longneck Buds. I have to admit, it felt instantly better to be outdoors, less claustrophobic, safer somehow. Overlooking his yard, concealed from the rest of the street by a cast-iron fence overgrown with oleanders blooming in pink and white, we sipped our beers in silence for a moment as the slow summer dusk began to close in and I groped for some way to get to what I'd come for.

"So Travis," I asked at last, trying my damnedest to make the question sound casual, "met any of your neighbors yet?"

"A few," he smiled. "They're decent enough, I suppose. The only neighbor I haven't met is the woman next door, and she's the only one who seems even vaguely interesting."

Damn it! "Hannah Winder," I said.

"You know her?"

I shrugged, sipping from my bottle. "It's a small town. Everybody knows everybody."

Travis must've seen something in my eyes, some spark of anger I couldn't smother. He turned and faced the lengthening blue shadows in the yard, the roses nodding along his back fence, then tipped up his beer and drained it.

"Want another?" he asked, seeing mine empty as well.

"Sure. Thanks."

He got up and went to the kitchen, so I had a moment to recover. I took a deep breath and tried to steady myself. Clearly, he was interested in Hannah—who wouldn't be?—but there wasn't a damn thing I could do about it. It wasn't my style to threaten the man; besides, I could tell it wouldn't do any good.

After a moment, he returned, took his seat on the steps with a weary groan, and handed me an ice-cold bottle.

"I'm drinking all your beer," I managed to say.

"That's what beer's for, Nick."

His voice took on a self-ironic, lecturing tone when he said that, and I couldn't suppress a chuckle. Frustrated, I found myself liking the guy. I hadn't intended to.

But I needed to rattle his cage, at least a little, so I reached into my shirt pocket, drew out a joint, and held it in front of him, curious to see how he'd react.

"Is that what I think it is?"

"Uh-huh." I was pleased to see that I'd caught him off guard. "Interested?"

Travis smiled slowly. "Why not?"

So I dug into my jeans pocket for the matches, lit the joint, and passed it across to him, disappointed in how readily he'd consented. I was hoping he'd be morally outraged and act like an asshole so I could look down on him, but Travis handled himself just fine. He pulled the THC-laden smoke greedily into his lungs like a pro, held it without coughing, and exhaled a blue cloud that hovered around his graying temples.

"You've done this before," I commented.

He laughed. As I watched, his expression softened dreamily, and that foolish, self-absorbed grin well known to dope-smokers slowly appeared on his face. Pleased, I grinned back at him.

"What?" he asked, perplexed.

I shook my head. "Nothing. Hey, don't Bogart."

He passed the joint back to me. I think he'd forgotten he had it. "Man," he sighed, "I haven't been high in years."

Travis picked up a shell that was lying on the steps and turned it absently in his fingers.

It was about two inches long, bands of sea-gray and what

looked like ivory beadwork spiraling down, tapering to a needle point that seemed dipped in blood. Drawing on the joint, I searched for a moment and came up with the name: *auger*. I thought of the steel version I carried in my toolbox.

Auger: a tool for boring into wood.

Augury: to penetrate the future, to delve beneath the surface.

"So what brings you to Galveston, Travis?"

"My God," he laughed, shaking his head ruefully, "a whole *series* of disasters."

"Yeah?"

He leaned back, as if to consider me from a greater distance, and I saw the decision, once he made it, on his face. People often trust me with their secrets; I'm not sure why. Maybe I'm a good listener, or maybe it's something they see in my demeanor, some combination of empathy and discretion, an appealing combination for someone with a weighty story to unload. I passed him the joint, and he paused to hit it. A blue thread of smoke curled from the end.

"I was an architect," he began. Then, "I guess I still am," he added, as if the thought had just occurred to him. "When I first got out of school, I was considered a very promising young man. When you're young, and everybody says things like that about you, it's hard not to let it go your head, you know?"

I nodded, though nobody had ever seen me that way.

"I was dating a woman whose father ran a successful architectural firm in St. Louis, and when we got married, I went to work for her daddy. Things were good for a while, a long while, actually. God knows, the money was rolling in. I thought I was gonna be the next Frank Lloyd Wright."

The comment about the money tipped me off to something I'd noticed but couldn't put my finger on. Travis was rich, or at least he had been. There was something in the way he carried himself, a leisurely grace, chin high, which suggested someone who'd grown accustomed to a certain level of privilege.

"So where does the tragic part come in?" I wanted to know.

Even stoned, Travis caught my sarcasm. Like a lot of working people, I operated on the assumption that rich folks don't *have* problems, not real ones, anyway. He smiled at me and passed back the joint.

"I reached that point in my life," he said, "when I wasn't really young anymore, and it wasn't good enough to be promising. It was time to fulfill my promise, if I was going to. I struggled with that for a while, but to make a long story short, I was eventually forced to recognize that I was nothing more than a competent craftsman." After a pause, he added, "I didn't have a thought in my head that I hadn't taken from someone else."

I knew what he was saying, of course, and I felt for him; but I hadn't come to that crossroads in my own life yet. I still had my illusions.

"What did you do?"

To my surprise, he grinned. "I set my life on fire."

In my mind, I saw a white house on a hill in flames, people running. I took a last hit and offered Travis what was left of the joint. He pinched it between his thumb and first finger, sucked up a final bit of smoke, and pitched it neatly into the yard. It arced through the twilight and landed on the grass, where it glowed for an instant like a firefly before going out.

"Julie couldn't begin to grasp my unhappiness," he went on. "As far as she was concerned, we were having a great success—living in the best neighborhood, frequenting the best restaurants. After a while, she wouldn't even talk to me about it. So I had an affair." He looked across at me. "You know, Nick, it's truly amazing how many men think they can remake their lives simply by sleeping with another woman."

I had no response to that. My own life had changed completely when I'd met Hannah, so I understood the impulse, the hope. "What happened?" I prompted him.

"There was some woman in the office, the kind who likes married men. You know the type?"

Again I nodded, but the truth is, I've never worked in an office in my life. I envisioned rows of desks beneath fluorescent lights, sleek predatory women in suits with bare legs and spike heels gliding sinuously past file cabinets, reading reports and exuding sexual promise.

"One night, we were working late, just the two of us. I looked at her and thought, why the hell not? There wasn't much worth saving at home. Julie found out, of course, and she got a lawyer. We didn't have any kids, so there were no innocent victims—only guilty ones. Her friends and family closed ranks around her, and I was practically ridden out of town on a rail." He shrugged. "It was just as well. Everything was used up for me there."

"So you slept with this woman *once*, and that was it?"

Travis smiled. "That was all it took."

I was secretly pleased at how much I'd gotten out of a few leading questions. Obviously, Travis had been alone with his thoughts for a while.

"But why here?" I asked. When he looked puzzled, I added, "What brought you to Galveston?"

"This was my grandparents' place." He gestured over his shoulder at the house hulking in the darkness at our backs. "It's been empty since their deaths, years ago. I spent a summer here when I was six. The odd thing is, for years I couldn't remember a damn thing about the island, the house, the time I spent here—as if three months of my life had never happened. Do you believe that's possible, Nick, to forget something so completely?"

"Sure, I guess so. If there's a reason to forget."

He regarded me in silence, considering this. Then he went on.

"After the divorce, I did some consulting in Dallas for a few months, and I started having dreams about this place. Just bits and pieces at first, carved porches with their lights on at night, things like that, but then the pieces began to connect, and I knew I had to come here. I've remembered even more since I arrived."

It was nearly dark by then, and his face in profile was a silhouette. Maybe the weed was making me suggestible, but I felt the house behind us listening.

"The first morning I was here," he said, "I saw my grandfather."

There was brief delay before the import of what he'd said hit home. Crickets droned steadily, eerily, in the grass, and a sense of unreality stole over me. I couldn't quite believe what I'd heard. He turned to watch my reaction, and I could see that he was absolutely serious.

"Saw him where?"

"Standing on the sidewalk, staring up at me. I was looking out of the window in the tower room. By the time I got to the front veranda, he was gone." After a moment, he added, "I think he *wanted* me to see him. In fact, I'm sure he did."

"Why?"

Travis tipped back his bottle and drained the last of his beer. "To scare me off. He never wanted me around, even when I was a kid. He hated me for some reason. And he doesn't like it one goddamn bit that I've come back."

What he was suggesting was so unlikely, so outrageous, that I couldn't form a response. The stillness of twilight, the in-between time, ended suddenly, the night announced by a breeze that rustled through the ragged bed of old roses along his back fence. Travis lapsed into silence, and he suddenly seemed far away, unreachable. I took it as my cue to go.

III

But I couldn't leave it at that. Travis Karlson actually believed that his dead grandfather stalked the neighborhood and wanted him gone. I needed to understand how someone—an apparently self-possessed, intelligent man, an *educated* man—could reach a conclusion like that. It was two days after our first meeting, and I'd come back for more.

It wasn't hard to prompt him. As Travis spoke, we passed the tightly rolled, pencil-thin joint back and forth between us like a pledge, his to speak, mine to listen. The crickets made a shrill, inhuman music as the dusk deepened around us in subtle, nearly indistinguishable gradations. The pink and white blossoms on the oleanders walling in his backyard glowed as if they'd drawn the last light into themselves.

"He didn't like me watching him," Travis began. "He'd call me *sneak*, little sneak. Never once called me by my name. He was a carpenter, a damn good one. One day, he was working in the backyard of a place down the street, building a deck. He stood bent over from the waist, with a row of three-penny nails in his mouth and a claw hammer in his hand, working his way along a row of two-by-fours. He'd take a nail from his mouth, position it, and drive it through the wood into the supporting beam with two *hard*, precise strikes—nail after nail. He never missed. I was watching him from behind a hedge at the border of the yard." He flashed me that brief, self-ironic smile. "I was fascinated by such directed violence. There was a kind of poetry to it, you know?"

I squinted at him through the smoke.

"When he ran out of nails, he reached into the pocket of the canvas apron at his waist for more and lined them up in his mouth. That's when he looked up and spotted me."

"What did you do?"

Travis laughed uneasily. "I froze like a rabbit. He stood there glowering at me, the brim of his hat pulled low, his shirt soaked with sweat, the hammer gripped in one hand. He was *furious*, Nick, beside himself with anger. My god, you should've seen him!"

The strange thing is, I *could* see him. I pictured him standing there, tense with rage, the glare of his lenses obliterating his eyes, a row of nails gleaming in his mouth.

"Want another beer?"

I did. Travis stood, opened the screen door, and stepped into the kitchen behind us.

When he opened the refrigerator, the pale ghost of the kitchen door appeared briefly on the darkening lawn at my feet. He settled on the step with two bottles and handed me one. I took a long, greedy pull, letting the cold brew slide down my throat, then asked him my question.

"Why would he mind you watching him? I mean, a lot of grandparents would be pleased, flattered that a kid was interested. What the hell was his problem?"

He never blinked. "He had some secret, something he'd done, and it twisted him out of shape. I think he was afraid I'd find out what it was."

"Did you?"

"No," he replied. "To this day, I still don't know. That's why he's still around, standing guard. Whatever it was, it must've been something god-awful. He brooded over it, hoarded it. I think he relived it constantly."

"How do you know *that*?"

Again that cool grin. "Because I caught him at it."

It was nearly dark by then. All I could see around us where we hunched side by side on his back steps was the vague outline of flowers: oleanders at intervals like stars lining the borders of the yard, the larger, heat-exhausted roses drooping along the back fence. I brushed a mosquito away from my face and waited for his explanation. The idea of any man, dead or alive, keeping watch over a private obsession intrigued me.

"One night, I woke up late with the feeling that something was happening outside. It was perfectly still, silent, but I *knew* there was something going on, and I had to know what it was.

There must've been a full moon that night, with clouds moving in off the Gulf, because my room kept going from a silvery brightness, almost as clear as day, to complete darkness and back again. I got out of bed and went to the window overlooking the backyard."

I *saw* it: moonlight crawled across the bedroom window, shining on the cool skin of the glass. The boy stepped carefully across the creaky wooden floor, but by the time he'd covered the short distance to window, it had gone dark again. Grasping the sill in both hands, he lifted up on tiptoes to look out . . .

"What did you see?" I asked.

"It was my grandfather, standing absolutely still at the edge of the rose garden."

The moon flew out of the bank of clouds blown in from the sea, and light draped suddenly across the old man's shoulders.

"What was he doing out there?"

Travis smiled. "That's what *I* wanted to know. He was standing with his back to the house, but I knew it was him. That gray sweater vest, the collar of his denim work shirt, his white hair spilling from the back of that dark, battered fedora he always wore."

Clouds swallowed the moon, but the figure remained in the darkness, frozen in space, unnerving in his concentration.

"Well," Travis went on, his voice low and steady, "I guess I don't have to tell you I was scared witless of the old man. But I understood at once that I was seeing something secret, something purposely hidden, and I couldn't very well turn away and go back to sleep. So I went downstairs, down the black throat of that staircase, and through the dining room to the kitchen. When I got to there, the moon broke through again. He'd left the back door open, pulled back to the wall, and I saw him framed in the screen door. He hadn't budged an inch. I could see the roses, pink in the moonlight, spread out at his knees."

As he spoke, I looked out at the rose garden, the flowers

erased now in the deep Gulf night. There were stars above the gabled back roof, above the window where the secretive, frightened boy had spotted the old man in the yard below.

"The screen was unlatched, so I pushed it open and stepped outside, catching the door so it wouldn't bang shut behind me. I had my eyes glued to his back, alert to any sign that he'd heard me, and I started toward him across the grass."

I imagined the boy passing silently between us where we sat on the steps, saw him creep across the damp grass, shoulders hunched—*three steps, six steps, nine . . .*

"He never moved. When I got nearer I could hear him whispering, muttering something, but I couldn't make out the words. I remember thinking he was talking to the roses." He smiled across at me uneasily in the dark. "I tried to get closer, to hear what he was saying. And that's when he knew I was there."

"What did he do?"

"All of a sudden he got still, completely silent. Then his head turned, slowly, and he glared down at me over his left shoulder. What I saw on his face was terrifying. I can't describe it." After a moment Travis added, "Have you ever seen anyone lost?"

"What do you mean *lost*?"

"Lost," he repeated with a shrug, holding his empty palms up. "Beyond the reach of any kind of hope or decency, any humanity. At that instant, that's where he was. You could see it in his eyes."

That, I admit, I couldn't picture, not precisely. Perhaps it was just as well.

"He would've killed me if he'd caught me then," Travis continued. "I have absolutely no doubt about that. I sprinted for the back door, and he was right behind me. I burst into the kitchen, slipped through the dining room, and pounded up the stairs, and when I got to the top, my grandmother was coming out of her room, wrapping herself in a housecoat. 'What on earth is going on?' she wanted to know. I glanced behind me, practically feeling the old man's fingers at my throat, and her eyes followed mine. He stood at the bottom of the stairs, leaning forward, a banister grasped in each hand as if he were about to leap to the top, those gray eyes fixed on me."

Travis paused for a moment, staring into the twilight, before he went on. "But the tension drained out of him, the rage, as soon as he saw his wife standing behind me. She'd put a hand on my shoulder, and I knew at once that I was safe."

He leaned forward, silent, elbows on his knees, hands locked together under his chin.

I finished the last of my beer, perplexed, and set the bottle at my feet. "How did you know *that*?" I asked him. "I mean, what would've prevented him from coming up those stairs, shoving her aside, and going after you? He doesn't sound like the kind of man who would've had any qualms about hurting a kid. Or a woman."

"That's true," he agreed. "But he would've never hurt me in front of her. *Never*. She was his lifeline, his connection to some kind of normal life, and he was afraid of losing that. He was already in hell," he added, turning to eye me with a blank, humorless smile, "but he knew there were lower levels."

THE NEXT DAY, I finished a job patching and painting the back porch of the Trube place on Sealy, an imposing stone house built in 1887 to fit the original owner's idea of what a German castle was supposed to look like. I worked in the shady, breeze-stirred back garden with the shadows of hanging lilac vines blowing across my labor. I was done by noon, and I had enough decent pine planking left over to replace the rotted front step on Bobbi Larkin's bungalow, as I'd promised I would. So I climbed into my old Ford F150, sun-faded from what had once been blue, and headed out there after lunch. Bobbi lived on the west end of the island, beyond the sea wall, with her Aunt Sally, a silent, continually smiling woman in her early sixties who, if anything, was even stranger than Bobbi.

From the time we were in grade school together, Bobbi Larkin had seen and heard things that other people were not tuned to receive. The visions that plagued her were not intermittent; they were like a tap she could not quite turn off, a nearly constant trickle, liable to flow again at any moment. They increased in clarity and intensity as she became a teenager, and at sixteen, Bobbi was hospitalized with a psychotic break. I was with her when the ambulance came to school to get her, and I have a vivid memory of the paramedic sliding the needle into her arm to stop her from screaming.

When Bobbi got out of the hospital, she hooked up with her Aunt Sally, a family eccentric with the supposed "gift" of second sight. With the help of her aunt, Bobbi learned how to cope with her unwanted distractions. Now she and her Aunt Sally occupied year-round a beach house on the sparsely populated west end of the island, subsisting on disability payments and picking up part-time jobs under the table. They didn't have much money, so I did odd jobs for them for free when I could fit them in.

Bobbi was an outsider. That was the connection between us, I guess. I've always had the habit of picking up strays.

So I drove along the seawall until it ended and the road dropped to the flat stretch of sand on the west end of the island. To my left, beyond the dunes, I caught glimpses of the gunmetal flash of the Gulf of Mexico. Clusters of brightly colored umbrellas sprang up like exotic mushrooms, marking the locations of the beach parks I passed. Making a left, I steered into a cluster of little houses raised on piers and rumbled slowly down the sandy, pot-holed street toward Bobbi's place. I pulled up in front of a weathered shoebox bungalow, steps rising to two sets of sliding glass doors, a second set of steps leading to a rooftop deck. A rusted anchor served as a centerpiece in her unkempt, ant-infested patch of front lawn.

I climbed the stairs, careful of the rotted one, and knocked. Aunt Sally appeared from the shadows in her green Wal-Mart housecoat and slid the door open a crack. Cold, air-conditioned air billowed in my face. When I informed her that I was going to replace the front step, she just smiled and nodded and closed the salt-stained glass door briskly in my face.

"You're welcome," I muttered.

But it was an easy job. I yanked out the rotted step with my hammer, measured and cut two pieces of pine, and nailed the new wood firmly into place. I was done in fifteen minutes.

It was Thursday, so I knew where Bobbi would be. Climbing into my truck, I headed west toward San Luis Pass, rolling down the window on the driver's side to breathe in the peppery, sun-broiled smell of the reeds and sea grass lining the road. I slowed down to move through Jamaica Beach—the cops there make a small fortune on tourists who barrel through town—and spotted the Seaview Grocery up ahead on the left. Pulling into the gravel lot, I soon emerged from the humid salt air into fluorescent lights and air-conditioning, asking the teenage girl at the checkout counter where Bobbi was. She nodded toward the back of the store, her greasy blonde ponytail wagging behind her. Her eyes widened and a little grin, mocking and conspiratorial, flickered across her face.

Fuck you, kid, I thought. I didn't like some know-nothing high school bitch laughing at my friend. But I said nothing. No point in making trouble for Bobbi. The Seaview had been willing to pay her under the table so she wouldn't lose her disability.

I found her at the back of Aisle Three, stocking the shelves with canned soup from cases of it she'd loaded on a dolly. Hearing me approach, Bobbi turned from her work—a shock of red hair under the fluorescent lights, piercing green eyes peering at me from either side of a thin, hooked nose. The tee shirt and men's cotton shorts she wore, too big for her, hung loosely on her angular frame. She seemed alarmed at first, tense, but her shoulders relaxed a little when she recognized me.

"Crap," she commented, rubbing her forehead with the heel of one hand, "I've known all day there was bad news coming. I didn't think it would come from you."

"How are you, Bobbi?"

"The same," she shrugged. "What do you want, Nickie?"

Bobbi didn't mean to be rude; she'd never had the chance to develop a knack for small talk, and I was used to her directness. Clearly, she was worried, and she wanted to know why I was there. That threw me. I really hadn't come with an agenda.

"Nothing. I fixed your step. Thought I'd drive out and see how you were doing."

She reached for a can of tomato soup and placed it neatly on the shelf, label out. "But something's happened, hasn't it?" she insisted, not looking at me. "Why don't you quit yanking my chain and tell me what it is."

Like most people, I assumed that problems like Bobbi's were related to brain chemistry and could be controlled with drugs. Better living through chemistry. Still, I had to admit, Bobbi Larkin had a way of picking up on things you hadn't told her. I knew from experience that it was useless trying to keep anything from her.

"Well," I began, stumbling into an explanation, "there's this guy in town who's fixing up a house. I went by to see him a few days ago. You know, try and drum up some business. He's been telling me some very strange stories."

I didn't mention anything about Hannah. I figured I had a right to my private life. My grief was my own concern.

"What stories?"

"He lived in that house for a while when he was a kid, and he claims his dead grandfather is hanging around the place and doesn't want him there."

I can't tell you how odd it felt to say that out loud, especially there, in the prosaic glare of the grocery store, surrounded by shelves of canned soup and packaged blue boxes of macaroni and cheese. I'd glanced down the aisle when I spoke, making sure we were alone, keeping my voice low so no one in the adjoining aisles could hear us. When I looked back, Bobbi was regarding me, her head tipped to one side, a kink in her right eyebrow.

"Do you believe what he's telling you?"

Belief was a tough one for me. "I'm not sure. *He* believes it, I can tell you that much. He may be deluded, but he's not lying. For one thing, the stories are too detailed."

"So how come you never believed *me*?"

Her question caught me off guard. Truth is, I wasn't sure I believed Travis, but I *did* take him seriously, no question about that. He was calm, self-possessed, accomplished; Bobbi, on the other hand, in her ill-fitting clothes, with her habit of tipping her head to one side to stare at you like a heron spotting its prey in the tide, was clearly a bit of an oddball. But it was more than that. Back in high school, I'd been with Bobbi a few times when she'd had an episode. What she made you feel at those moments was her *fear*, her abject terror, but never the cause of it.

"How can I believe in something I can't see?" I said, defending myself. This was an old argument between us. "In something I find no *evidence* for?"

"You're lucky." Bobbi aimed a dour half-smile at me. "Stay blind, Nickie. You'll be happier that way."

But that, I realized, was the problem. I wasn't really blind anymore, not completely. Whether I liked it or not, Travis was making me see.

"There's still something you're not telling me," Bobbi insisted.

I didn't know what she meant at first.

She added, "There's a girl involved, a woman."

"You're the only girl for me," I responded evasively.

"Horse crap, Nickie," Bobbi countered, but she was smiling.

"Don't try to sweet talk me. Remember, I know how full of shit you are." Then her face grew suddenly serious, and she jammed a thin index finger in my face. "You're gonna have to watch out for her, and for that kid of hers, too—whether you want to or not."

I said nothing. That was fine with me.

Bobbi went back to stacking cans, and I moved aside to let a shopper on her way to the meat counter squeeze past with her cart. When she was gone, Bobbi paused, a can in one hand, and regarded me quizzically for a moment before she spoke.

"If you never believed me, if you thought I was just some crazy bitch, why did you visit me when I was in the hospital? You know, you were the only one in that entire goddamn high school who ever did."

"We were friends," I shrugged.

Bobbi moved quickly, as if she'd been stung or slapped, bending over from the waist to fill her arms with soup cans. I was afraid at first that I'd offended her, but then I heard a stifled sob and realized that she was crying and didn't want me to know. I'm not the touchy-feely type—I leave that kind of stuff to the born-again Christians—but at that moment, my heart went out to her. I wanted to hug her, maybe rub her poor, bony shoulders for her, something. But I knew that Bobbi Larkin couldn't abide being touched.

"See you soon," I whispered, and started to inch away.

She jerked her head up, cans cradled against her chest, and froze me in my tracks. "You have *no idea* what you're getting into, do you? You watch your ass, Nickie. I don't have many goddamn friends. I can't afford to lose any."

We looked at each other for a moment, her brimming green eyes boring into me, and I could see at once that she was serious. Disconcerted, I stepped away down the aisle, heading for the exit and the sane, familiar sunlight skating over the asphalt road.

IV

BOBBI'S WARNING DISTURBED ME more than I wanted to admit, and I stayed away from Travis's ramshackle Queen Anne monstrosity for a week or so. I was determined to keep my feet planted firmly on the ground, and I told myself that the things he'd said *couldn't* be true, that I'd let myself be taken in by someone who was either delusional or an outright liar. At night, after losing myself all day as well as I could in some repair job, hanging drywall or restoring the convoluted intricacies of an Eastlake paint job, I'd make it a point to stay away from his place, settling deliberately on my couch and listening to Steve Earle or maybe some old Grateful Dead tunes. But it was too late: I was already woven into the fabric of the story he was spinning, and I couldn't get it out of my mind.

And worse, I soon realized that Travis's detailed yarns and the possibilities they presented had had an advantage beyond their power to intrigue: they'd distracted me from the heartache I felt over losing Hannah. Left on my own, I found that pain crashing down on me again with a renewed, sickening force. I couldn't stand it.

So, partly out of curiosity, partly out of cowardice, I went back to see how the rest of the story played out. I showed up at his place after work one day with a six-pack of cold Carta Blancas under my arm. It was August 9, the day before the rain hit, and it was the last session of this kind that Travis and I had together.

I stepped through the gate and found him crouched on his knees in the patch of front yard, covering with a thick coat of forest-green enamel the shutters he'd taken down and lined up along the base of the house. Hearing me approach, he whipped around nervously to glare at me over his shoulder, and the expression on his face stopped me where I stood. It was a raw look, his momentary alarm tempered by an even stronger determination to face down whatever threatened him—to attack, if need be, in self-defense. That look softened as soon as he saw that it was me, but I'd seen it clearly, and I knew at once what it meant.

"Travis, what's happened?"

To my surprise, I found my skepticism comprised at once. *Something* was happening to this man; whatever it was, to him it was utterly real.

"Hey, Nick," he said, ignoring my question, still on his knees. "I thought you'd forgotten about me."

As Travis got to his feet, I made some lame excuse about having been busy, but I felt guilty as hell. I was the only one he could talk to about the things that had happened to him, that *were* happening to him. We'd entered into an unspoken agreement, and I'd let him down by not showing up. As I was about to discover, he was anxious to talk.

He led me through the house, and moving past the front parlor, I noticed that he'd managed to get that pocket door down by himself somehow and lowered across a pair of sawhorses. On top of the door, his electric sander perched like an enormous rat, its cord trailing off like a tail.

We were soon settled in our usual spot on the steps, Travis to my left, each of us clutching a cold Carta Blanca. An awkward silence followed, and I realized he was waiting for me to speak, to question him. That was the price, I guess, of having stayed away. So we talked for a few minutes about his work on the house, and then I asked him again.

"Something's happened, hasn't it? I could see it on your face a minute ago."

Travis turned to me, pale under the eyes, his expression an echo of the one I'd seen earlier. I must've satisfied him about my defection. He came right to the point.

"I was sanding down that pocket door in the front parlor this morning, and when I looked up from my work for a second, *there he was*—standing on the front porch, right up against the window."

I didn't have to ask who.

Travis shook his head, bewildered. "But this time it wasn't halfway down the block through the hand-blown glass of that leaded window in the turret. He was right on the porch, not ten feet away, pushing up against the glass and staring in at me with those cold gray eyes. He was *watching* me. It wasn't like some film being replayed, you know—he knew I was there." Travis glanced across at me, wanting to be sure I understood the distinction. "I could see every line on his face. Instinctively, I'd turned the sander off, and as I met that stare, the *silence* dawned on me—no birds, no cicadas. Absolute dead silence, as if his standing there had blotted out the world."

The image filled me with dread. I saw the old man crowding against the house, his eyes like stone, framed in the window like a sepia portrait.

"After a few seconds," Travis continued, "he turned and walked away, and the sound of birds rushed back. I was cold, shaky; it took me a minute to work up the grit to go out on that porch. But when I did, it was empty, and there was no one in the yard. Or the street, either."

A breeze stirred through the overgrown arms of oleander, rustling everything around us in the twilight.

"Jesus Christ, Travis," I muttered.

"Tell me about it," he grinned nervously. "When you came up behind me earlier, I thought he was back."

With a sudden, self-serving clarity, I recognized my opportunity. I liked Travis, but I wanted him gone. "Why in the world do you stay here?" I asked him. "I mean, if it was me, I'd pack up and get the hell off the island. Why are you subjecting yourself to this?"

He responded without a pause. "This is *my* house. It belongs to me now. After the divorce, it's about all I have left. Besides," he added, turning to meet my eye, "I'm not six years old anymore. I won't be driven off by that man."

He's not a man, I wanted to tell him. *Not anymore*. But I kept my observation to myself.

Walking home under the black spreading branches of the live oaks, I could hear the traffic rushing behind me on Broadway, and under that, faintly, the steady, rhythmic breath of the Gulf of Mexico, felt in the blood more than heard. It was clear Travis wasn't leaving, so I figured I'd drop by every few days and keep an eye on him, maybe find some means to keep him away from Hannah. I thought I could watch and listen safely, from a distance. I didn't understand yet that I was already part of the story.

IT RAINED FOR SEVERAL DAYS after that. The first tropical depression of the season dropped a steady, salt-scented downpour on the island, flooding the streets of the East End before the storm broke up and moved north. When Travis emerged at last from the house, late in the afternoon, it was too wet to paint, so he decided to tackle the rose garden in his backyard. He wanted to clean up the bed before the weeds choked out the flowers, maybe shovel in some fresh soil and peat moss.

That's when he first met Ruby. She has a way of appearing suddenly at the edge of your vision, obeying an impulse to come at things obliquely, from an angle. I imagine Travis looking up from his work to find the child standing there as if she'd sprung up from the ground, watching him silently with her mother's dark eyes.

"What're you doing?" Ruby wanted to know.

Her pale faced was framed in dark auburn hair. She wore a vivid green tee shirt, denim pedal pushers, and red sneakers. He recognized her, of course, from seeing her come and go next door.

"I'm gonna pull out these weeds so the roses can breathe better," he replied. "Try to make the flowers come back like when I was a boy."

"Oh, that's okay. She'll like that."

As he worked, Travis regarded her furtively. "Who?"

"The woman who lives in the roses," Ruby responded, matter-of-fact. She was impatient with the denial she expected. She was used to having her perceptions discounted.

I'm not sure what Travis actually thought of her remark, but when he nodded and didn't contradict her, a bond began to develop between them. The two regarded each other closely, a hesitant smile of recognition flickering over both their faces. Unlike her mother, this grownup made no attempt to dismiss what Ruby said or to tell her she was imagining things. And Travis, considering his neighbor's silent, abstracted daughter, saw a version of the secret-burdened child he'd been, in this same place, at her age.

"What's your name?" he asked her.

"Ruby," she replied, as if the answer were obvious. Unconsciously, she brushed a stray honeybee away from her face.

"That's a pretty name."

The little girl nodded seriously. She thought so, too.

So they talked, and Hannah, looking out her kitchen window, spotted her daughter with the man next door, a man she still didn't know. In Hannah's eyes, Ruby's fatherlessness surrounded her like an aura, marking her, making her more vulnerable than other children; and though Hannah tried hard to ignore it, she also suspected that Ruby *saw* things, things like Hannah had seen slogging through the mud in her father's ruined cornfield. So she was constantly on guard when it came to her child.

Well then, if Ruby was going to strike up a friendship with the newcomer, Hannah intended to find out who he was. Besides, she saw at once the opportunity her daughter had unwittingly created. She had every reason, now, to go over and present herself—any parent *would* have—and she could do so in the man's backyard, away from the prying eyes of her neighbors. As I've said, Galveston in many ways is still a small Southern town, and as a single woman, Hannah needed to be careful about her reputation.

So she creaked through the gate that connected their yards and emerged from between the flowering stands of oleander. Hannah approached, smiling but wary, bemused to see her normally silent little girl chattering away with a total stranger.

"Well Ruby," she said, folding her arms across her chest, "I see you've made a new friend."

Travis got to his feet, the knees of his blue jeans wet from the ground, and wiped the earth from his hands. "Hello," he smiled. "You must be Ruby's mother."

The little girl turned to watch the grownups regard each other.

Hannah grasped the hand he offered, and Travis took her in with a glance, completely, without appearing to do so—the woman he'd watched from a distance for the past three weeks or so. Her light brown hair, the color of tarnished and finger-loved brass, was unpinned, hanging loosely down her back, the office clothes traded in for an old pair of faded blue jean cut-offs and a soft cotton tee shirt. Any man alive would've been impressed. They exchanged names, a little small talk, and then Hannah invited him over for coffee.

From that point on, it was only a matter of time.

Travis followed her willingly, Ruby at his side looking up at him, already half in love in the sudden way of children. Once seated at Hannah's kitchen table, they talked some more, probably about Ruby, who by then was down the hall in the television room, watching the cartoons that seemed to be her one distraction. Hannah probed him for his background as I had done. She's one of the least mercenary women I've ever known, an especially rare quality in a woman as attractive as she is, since beauty always confers choices. But she looked at every man she met as a potential father for Ruby, and the unmistakable air of privilege given off by her new neighbor impressed her. At some point, the coffee was exchanged for the bottle of tequila Hannah kept in the cupboard, and then she insisted he stay for dinner.

I can picture Travis Karlson sitting at her kitchen table, the light from the overheads sparkling and flashing from the effects of the tequila, Ruby, returned now, counting out the greasy, dog-eared cards for a game of Old Maid while Hannah bustled at the stove, frying beef and chopping lettuce and tomatoes for tacos. After so many nights spent alone in that bleak, musty old house with all its nightmares, Travis must've felt like one lucky sonofabitch.

On principle, she wouldn't have slept with him the first time they met; but if Hannah liked Travis, and I know she did, she wouldn't have wasted any time in letting him know. At some point, they wound up in Hannah's brass bed, under the blue and red patchwork comforter her grandmother had stitched together, a place I once thought belonged exclusively to me.

Suspecting nothing, I showed up at Travis's place on the evening of August 14, a date that's engraved in my memory. I'd come to help him get the massive pocket door from his front parlor refitted on its runner.

When I arrived, I could sense right away that something had happened, but I didn't know what. There was a weight of intrigue in the air, a self-satisfied smile on Travis's face that he didn't seem anxious to explain. As we struggled with the awkward slab of wood, tipping it gently from the sawhorses to get it in place, a knock came at the screen door in the kitchen. Gingerly, we laid the eight-foot hunk of teak against the wall, and Travis went to see who was there.

"Hey, miss me?" a voice asked.

I'd stayed in the parlor, holding the door to make sure it didn't slip. From where I stood, I couldn't see into the kitchen, but I recognized the voice; and from the question itself, as well as from the tone, I understood at once what had happened. I felt as if I'd been kicked in the gut by a mule.

"Nick's here," Travis warned her. "Come and say hello."

A brief pause ensued, and I pictured questioning glances exchanged out of sight. Then Travis came through the dining room with Hannah right behind him, her eyes down, hooking a strand of hair behind one ear. I hadn't seen her in weeks, but her effect on me, I noticed, hadn't lessened one bit.

"Hello, Nick," she said, forcing a smile, the strain audible beneath her attempt to sound nonchalant. "I heard you were doing some work over here."

And so have you, I thought sullenly.

I smiled back and nodded. Hannah's eyes, the color of bitter chocolate, locked briefly on mine and dropped to the floor. Travis watched this exchange in silence; whatever suspicions he'd nursed about Hannah and me must've been confirmed for him instantly. The atmosphere of the room was electric with unspoken feelings; it was hard to breathe.

Mercifully, the phone in the kitchen rang, momentarily breaking the tension, and Travis excused himself to answer it, leaving me with the door balanced against my shoulder and Hannah's eyes on me.

"So, you and Travis, huh?"

I tried to sound casual, but she must've read the expression on my face. I felt raw, flayed alive.

"It was over between you and me, Nick."

"Not for me, it wasn't."

Well, the cat was out of the goddamn bag. Hannah stumbled back as if I'd slapped her. I guess, in a way, I had. At the very least, I'd driven a knife into the heart of our little fiction about being friends. She turned to go, so briskly that the hair swept across her back. I caught the brief, familiar scent of her perfume, and I hated that she wasn't wearing it for me. As Travis was stepping back into the room, she touched him once on the arm, the gesture quick but intimate, and said, "Call me." The screen door in the kitchen banged shut behind her.

Ten seemingly endless minutes later, Travis and I managed to fit the casters into their tracks, and the eight-foot teak door was rolled back into its recess. We hadn't said a word to each other.

Furious, feeling betrayed by both of them, I pounded down the front steps into the green evening light, determined, now, to stay away for good. I had no intention of hanging around to witness their happiness.

And that might've been the end of the story, at least as far as I was concerned, if not for what happened next.

I had reached the bottom of the stairs and taken a step toward the gate and the street beyond. My thoughts, at that moment, were subsumed in bitterness and anger. All I wanted was to get as far away from that place as I could, as fast as I could, and hopefully never see either one of them again. I was sick of Travis's ghosts, and sick of my own, as well. But as I rushed for the street, my escape was suddenly halted.

A figure on the sidewalk stepped past the gate, moving in the space of a second from behind one hedge of oleander to the next. The smear of a blue shirt, some kind of vest, a hat. The man seemed formed out of the dusk—his face turning to me as he passed, gray eyes behind his lenses obscured in the shadow of his hat brim.

Then he was gone. It took me a moment to understand what I'd seen.

So *close*. Not fifteen feet away. I forced my hand to the iron gate, opened it, and stepped rigidly out onto the sidewalk.

The street, in the bruise-colored twilight, was deserted. A streetlight snapped on above the blackening shapes of live oaks.

V

BUT I KNEW WHAT I'D SEEN. The proximity of that *thing*, even in memory, was enough to turn me cold at the bone. In that brief instant at the gate, in the green, shadowy twilight, I'd felt the dead man's awareness, his *intent*, focused keenly on me.

The solid things around me seemed to lose their mass and take on the shimmering quality of a mirage. For days, what I'd seen moved unavoidably through my mind. To stop the scene repeating in my head, the face turning to regard me coolly, arrogantly, from under that hat-brim, I clutched at my anger. At least there was life in that. I brooded over Travis's betrayal and Hannah's guilty defection, imagining a plot where there wasn't one. It seemed to work; color and weight flowed back into the world. As I hung sheet rock or tried to trace the leak in a hundred-year-old plumbing system, I imagined the two of them together in Travis's bedroom at the top of the stairs. It was like pushing my tongue repeatedly against an aching tooth, but the pain was better than the alternative.

One evening at the end of August, I wandered down to the Strand to mix with the raucous mob of tourists spilling from the bars onto the sidewalk.

Music blared; there was a strained conviviality in the air, as if the visitors felt their summer ending and were determined, at all costs, to have some fun before they went home broke and sunburned. Shouldering my way through the boozy crowd, I imagined the nineteenth-century brick warehouses lining the streets submerged to their shattered second-story windows in a black, roiling sea, the glass broken out by hundred-and-twenty-mile-per-hour winds, the tide choked with the bodies of the very tourists bumping up against me—a staggering feeling, that sense of being touched by the dead. They screamed with laughter, unaware of the horror and repulsion I felt.

On the afternoon and evening of September 8, 1900, the entire island had been swallowed up for more than seven hours, submerged by a hurricane that had caught the city off guard. The enormous sand dunes to the east of town had been shoveled into wagons and carted away, allowing the growing population of Galvestonians easier access to the beach, so when the storm hit, there was nothing to stop it. By the time the novelty of the high waves and wind had worn off and people began to grasp their predicament, the railroad line and wagon bridges crossing the bay to the mainland were already under water. The city was trapped, and the sea continued to rise. The highest point on the island, along Broadway, was almost nine feet under water, and the wind tore the slate tiles from roofs and hurled them through the air like razors. Many of the people who died in that storm were decapitated or had an arm shorn off by a roof tile and bled out into the sea.

When the Gulf finally drew back, around ten o'clock that night, the island was covered with foul-smelling mud and debris. The next morning, survivors found the bodies of the drowned everywhere, face down in the mud or staring open-eyed at the sky. Over six thousand people had died, though it took the city fathers weeks to arrive at that figure. Houses in the East End had been spared by a wall of wreckage piled up against the Gresham place, a three-story stone mansion at Fourteenth and Broadway, now the Bishop's Palace. The barricade had kept the waves from tearing the houses apart, but I knew from experience that there wasn't an old home on the island that didn't have a high-water mark like a scar somewhere in its interior, usually on the second floor.

City authorities forced survivors to work burial details. The crews would go through the streets loading the dead onto wagons, stacking them like cordwood, a deputy with a shotgun standing over them to keep them at it, kerchiefs tied over their mouths and noses to block the smell. My great-great-grandfather Nicholas, the one who came over from Greece, was on one of those terrible crews. When the wagon was full, they took the bodies to a barge docked at the Twelfth Street Wharf and loaded them on board. Someone had found a barrel of whiskey, and for every wagonload, the crew-members were given a cup of liquor to keep them on their feet.

When the barge was full, they took the bodies out into the Gulf and dumped them.

But Galveston is a barrier island, and the same tides that had built it in the first place tossed the bodies back. The next morning, they washed in, rolled up horribly on the beaches, fish-eaten and covered with flies. Things got out of control then. People started dousing corpses with kerosene and burning them, burying them wherever they were found—no time for ceremony, no words said over the grave, no markers. The entire island, now, is little more than a muddy sandbar held in place by the bones buried on it.

So, walking the Strand that evening, past the crowded row of bars and tee shirt shops, this catalogue of disaster, known to me since I was a boy, rolled over me with a fresh force: six thousand people, probably more, all of them dead before their time. The city belonged to them.

I needed a drink, needed to drive all that death and decay from my mind, to wash the taste of the salt sea from my mouth. Sitting at the bar in one of those packed, noisy tourist joints, I met a woman named Sandra, or Sarah. It's hard to remember names after your third tequila. She was a redhead from the Midwest, a secretary, showing off her freckled shoulders and sunburned chest in a cornflower blue sundress.

My mind wasn't right. "Are you alive?" I asked her.

She looked at me strangely for a moment, but she must've figured I was only drunk.

"Let's find out," she grinned.

So we wound up at my place. The only thing I can recall with any clarity is how pale she was in those places covered by her swimsuit. The act that followed was swift and perfunctory; a little human heat, a quick twinge of pleasure, and it was over. But at least she restored me to the living. Then Sandra or Sarah pulled on her panties, stepped into her pretty blue dress, and left me to my misery, a single dull lamp burning in the dark house. More than likely, she went back to Nebraska and told her girlfriends how she'd slept with a pirate.

Alone again, I sat up against the wall, legs splayed to keep myself from falling over. My shoulder was against a window frame, and I could hear, outside the glass, the slow, desolate whistle of a freight train making its way across the black sheen of the bay to the mainland. Vaguely, through the fog of the alcohol, I realized I had weeks, maybe months, of suffering ahead of me, and there wasn't a damn thing I could do but endure it.

ON THE THURSDAY BEFORE Labor Day, my cell phone rang, and I switched off the circular saw to take the call. Travis was on the line. He said there was something he needed to show me, and I could tell from the hesitation in his voice, the way the words kept back more than they gave, that something drastic had happened. He asked me to come to the house as soon as I could. I was still pissed off, but staying away wasn't making things any better, so I told him I'd be there and hung up.

And so, that simply, I was drawn back in. At about six that evening, white with dust from the sheetrock I'd been cutting that day, looking for all the world like a ghost myself, I walked up his front steps. To my surprise, the nine-foot storm doors were bolted. I knocked, heard the latch slide, and a door swung out to admit me.

Travis and I stood in the slowly cooling shadow of the encaustic tile alcove, both of us silent. From between the warped pair of storm doors a little light leaked in. He jammed his hands into the pockets of his rumpled khakis, staring down meditatively, it seemed, to consider his scuffed brown loafers as he waited for my reaction. The front door was ripped from its jamb and leaning at a crazy angle against the wall, the beveled glass oval broken out.

"Christ, Travis. What the hell happened? Looks like someone kicked your door in."

He glanced up, meeting my gaze, but said nothing. Behind him, a single mosquito danced against the wall in the slant of evening light.

Perplexed, I turned back to the door.

That old house was solid, built to last, and I could see that none of the wood was rotted. It would've practically taken a battering ram to smash in that door, but strangely, the side of it that had faced the street was unmarked. It didn't make any sense.

I squatted down for a closer look. Not so much as a knick on the finish.

"Did you have a break-in?" I repeated.

No reply. Annoyed, I glanced up over my shoulder and found Travis studying me. "In a manner of speaking," he responded dryly.

"What the hell is that supposed to mean?"

Instead of answering my question, he picked his way carefully through the shards of glass littering the floor and stepped toward the staircase. "Let me show you something else," he called back to me.

So I followed him up the stairs, seething with impatience, and found him waiting in front of a bedroom door. The hall smelled like fresh paint and wood-stain. With a quick stab of panic, I realized that this was the first time I'd been drawn so far into the house. I didn't like it much. I felt exposed, visible from too many angles. The closed doors on the landing seemed shut on some presence waiting behind them, silent, listening in the stillness.

Travis tipped his head once at the door.

"What do you make of this?" he asked.

I ran my fingers over the rounded dents, the pale, splintered wood showing the marks plainly.

"Someone took a hammer to your door," I told him. That much was clear; what I couldn't figure out was why. My first thought was that a kid had done it, though it didn't seem like something Ruby would've done. Besides, the marks were above shoulder height, too high for a child to make—at least with enough force to scar the wood that way. The door was pretty well smashed up.

Again he was silent, watching me, gauging my reaction.

"Travis, are you gonna tell me what the fuck is going on here, or are we gonna play twenty questions?"

"Come to the kitchen," was all he said.

To my surprise, we found Hannah seated there, waiting for us. The hanging lamp above the table was switched on, casting a cone of white light in the slowly darkening room. Smiling to myself, I thought of one of those movies from the nineteen-forties where a team of detectives in silk suits interrogates some hardened criminal, a movie where everyone smokes. I knew at once that I'd been set up. Then I noticed Hannah's hands clutched tightly in front of her on the table. Over her shoulder, the back door had been left open and the screen unlatched, as if she were expecting to make a sudden exit. She was terrified to be there, and when I understood that, it was all I could do to keep from throwing my arms around her to comfort her. But that wasn't my place anymore.

"Hi Nick," she said, peeking up at me. "Thanks for coming."

She made it a point to keep her eyes on me when she said that so I'd know she meant it.

They wanted something. Resigned, I spilled into the chair to her left. Travis leaned in the doorway that connected to the dining room, his back to the gathering shadows.

"Okay," I said, "let's hear it."

They exchanged a quick look. "Go ahead," Hannah said, and Travis began, at last, to tell me what had happened.

It was after midnight, Hannah was asleep, and Travis was finishing the last of the Chianti from dinner. He was beginning to drowse over his book when a single crash, a sound like breaking glass and splintering wood, brought him instantly to his senses. Footsteps pounded up the stairs, and Travis reached instinctively for the crowbar he kept stashed under the bed. His hand had just closed over the iron when a crash shook the bedroom door in its frame. Hannah bolted upright, the hair in her eyes, and two of them stared, frozen with shock, as a series of blows smashed against the door. A pause ensued, and then Ruby's high-pitched scream sounded from the hallway. Hannah sprang out of bed, frantic to reach her daughter, but Travis held her back and threw the door open. They found Ruby, wide-eyed, standing in the hall. "There was a man with a hammer," she told them. Travis locked Hannah and Ruby in the master bedroom while he searched the house room by room. The place was empty, but he found the front door broken in; so he bolted the storm doors, and the three of them kept an uneasy vigil until morning.

"Where's Ruby now?" I wanted to know.

"She's at a friend's house," Travis replied. "She's fine."

"She's *not* fine!" Hannah broke in, slamming an open palm on the table, the frustration in her voice barely holding back the panic. "How could she be fine? She's only a little girl! How is she supposed to deal with *this*?"

Hannah wiped the tears from her eyes with the heel of one hand. We all knew what *this* meant, though none of us said it. Ruby had seen the old man; he was in the house now; his hammer marks scarred the bedroom door. With a groan, Travis lowered himself into the chair to my left.

"What do you intend to do?" I asked him.

As usual, he had a ready answer. "We can't stay in this house. Hannah can't," he corrected himself, "and neither can Ruby. So we're gonna move into Hannah's place. I'll continue to work here during the day. I intend to finish what I started." His gaze shifted briefly to mine when he said that, and I could see at once that he meant it. "I own this place outright," Travis added. "When the house is finished, when it's fixed up properly and really livable again, I can get four hundred and fifty grand for it, easy. I can't afford to walk away."

He was rehearsing this, I realized, for Hannah's sake, not mine. The money would bankroll a fresh start for the two of them. It was the hope she was holding out for. Well, that was fine for them, but where did I fit in?

"I'll be done in a few days," Travis continued. "Two weeks tops. All I really have left is the upstairs bedrooms. And repairing that front door, of course." He turned in his chair to face me and paused for a moment before he spoke. "Nick, I don't want Hannah or Ruby to be alone for an instant while I finish the job. We'd like you to move in with us for a week or so."

So that was it! I was literally stunned silent. How could they ask that of me? What the hell was I supposed to do, sleep on the couch in Hannah's front parlor while the two of them went at it in the bedroom down the hall? My disbelief had just given way to anger when I felt a slim palm fall on my forearm, and I turned to find Hannah leaning toward me across the table.

"Nick, please." She shook my arm lightly. "*Please*. If not for me, then for Ruby."

Her eyes fell on me with a weight that kept me in my seat. As I searched myself for a response strong enough to match my resentment, Bobbi's words came back to me with a fresh impact. *You're gonna have to watch out for her, and for that kid of hers, too—whether you want to or not*. That sealed it. I took a deep breath.

Against my better instincts, I agreed.

VI

AND SO BEGAN ONE of the oddest, most strained domestic arrangements I hope ever to endure. It lasted only six days, but it felt like six months. We avoided speaking of the haunting, afraid of lending it force with our words, and we kept our other feelings to ourselves, as well. But the unspoken subtexts grew for being ignored, as such things always do, until they filled the rooms and left us, it seemed, no air to breathe and nothing in common but our inarticulate bitterness and mutual suspicions.

One night, tossing on Hannah's couch, I saw myself falling through fog, gliding down like a seabird to a strip of beach obscured by shifting planes of white mist. I could hear surf and smell the salt water, and as my feet settled in the sand, I spotted a figure standing at the edge of the sea. A cloud billowed over the man, swallowing him, but I'd seen a rod and reel in his hand. Slowly, I felt my way forward, my bare feet moving over the cool, damp sand. The surf was invisible in the thick, feathery mist, but I heard the waves sloughing out over the sand and withdrawing again with hypnotic regularity. For an instant, I recognized the sound as my own breathing, and with that I nearly surfaced; but I needed to see the fisherman's face—it was urgent somehow that I do so—and I sank back seamlessly into the dream.

The man had not moved. He kept vanishing and reappearing in the swirl of fog as I stepped toward him. Finally, I stood only a few feet away.

He was dressed in layers of black rags—they fell over his back and arms in tatters like the feathers of a crow or a grackle. Approaching cautiously from the man's left, I tried to look at his face, but I saw only three or four days' worth of gray stubble. I passed behind him and looked from the other side; again, only a glimpse of the man's unshaved jaw, the rest of the face turned from me, staring out to sea. Then, with the sudden dislocation of a dream, I found myself standing directly in front of him as the mist curled over us.

It was Travis's face, the high forehead, the graying brown hair wet from the fog; but the eyes were blank, without pupils. Dread rushed over me—*the fisherman was blind*! Then, without warning, the pole jerked violently in his hands, and line began singing, running out. He had hooked something powerful. His grip tightened, and he stared out to sea with his stone eyes . . .

I woke with a start, drenched in sweat, and it took me several confused seconds to recognize the outline of Hannah's parlor, a window on either side of the door with its half-moon transom.

Then I remembered: I was sleeping on her couch.

A hand touched my arm.

"*Shhh!* Go back to sleep."

I could make out a form like a silhouette standing by the couch: the shape of a head, long hair, a ruffle of girlish night-gown at her throat.

"Ruby?" I muttered.

"You were having a bad dream," the child whispered. "It's okay. Go back to sleep."

How many times, I wondered, had her mother said those same words to her? I felt her leaning toward me, and before I understood what she was doing, Ruby had kissed me, once, on the forehead, and turned away. Her bare feet padded softly down the hall as she went back to bed.

Wide awake, I lay in the dark, listening to the air stir like the tide heard when you hold a shell to your ear.

LATE THE NEXT MORNING, four days into our uneasy cohabitation, Travis, Hannah, and I sat around the kitchen table, the remnants of breakfast smeared greasily on the plates we'd pushed aside. We were moodily silent, having run by that time through our brief store of small talk. Ruby, starting her third week of first grade, had been safely escorted to the bus for school, and now Travis absentmindedly reviewed the list of things he needed from Chalmers Hardware. Saying he'd be back in an hour, he left by the kitchen door and dashed through the rain for his Land Rover.

"Want another cup of coffee?" Hannah asked. The rain was hypnotic, insulating, adding a slight resonance or echo to her voice, as if she were speaking in a cave.

"Sure. Thanks."

She didn't have to ask how I took it. Pushing herself up from the table, Hannah poured two mugs from the pot on the counter, then stepped to the refrigerator for some milk to add to mine. She put the smoking mug in front of me and lowered herself into a chair.

"I've remembered something that happened to me when I was a girl," she said. "Something I'd forgotten for years." She held her chin in one hand, an elbow propped on the table, her eyes on the rain streaking the window. "Do you think we can do that, forget something on purpose—you know, scramble it? Something we don't want to deal with?"

I recalled, with a slight start, that Travis had once asked me that very question.

"Of course," I replied. The bitterness leaked into my voice before I could stop it. "People are wonderful at ignoring what they don't want to acknowledge."

Hannah caught my meaning and glanced away. Rain fell in the silence.

"I'm sorry, Nick," she offered at last, turning to face me. "We shouldn't have asked you to stay here. It's just that I'm so damned scared. How were we supposed to deal with what's going on? If we tried to tell anyone what was happening to us, anyone but you, they'd think we were crazy. We had no one else to turn to."

Tears welled in those fine eyes. I was angry at her, at both of them, but I felt like a bastard for making her cry.

"Tell me what you remembered," I coaxed, trying to make it up to her. I started to reach for her hand across the table but stopped myself.

A muted rumble sounded overhead, another squall line blowing in off the Gulf. When Hannah spoke, her voice was barely raised above a whisper, as if she were alone, talking to herself. I had to lean toward her to listen.

"I was fifteen that summer. A vulnerable age, especially for a girl who's grown up on a farm. I guess I was pretty innocent." She smiled and wiped away the tears with her index finger. "I was wandering in the woods one afternoon. It was so hot! I remember the cicadas were practically screaming in the trees. The wind was swirling, so the trees swayed, rustling, and the light and shadow moved, making everything fluid, unreal. Do you know what I mean?"

I nodded, sipping my coffee, and she went on.

"I'd stumbled into some place I didn't recognize, which surprised me. I thought I knew every inch of those woods. I made my way downhill through a stand of maple trees, skirting some briars, and stepped into a clearing."

For a moment, I saw the light and shadow flowing, heard a hot wind moving in the trees. Hannah paused, collecting herself with a nervous breath. Her eyes met mine for an instant, then flicked away.

"There was an old shack against the line of trees," she added. "Then suddenly there were two men standing there."

"What do you mean, *suddenly*?"

"I stepped into the clearing," Hannah repeated, a hand to her brow, seeing it. "There was some tumbledown shack I'd never seen before. Nobody around. And then there were two men there."

I saw them: ragged; colorless and dusty as sparrows.

"You mean they came out of the shack," I offered uneasily. "Or stepped out of the woods or something."

"No, they didn't," she insisted, shaking her head, smiling weakly. "I was looking straight ahead. One instant they weren't there, and the next they were. Two men. They looked like they'd been left out in the rain for a long, long time."

Hannah stared past the storm-blurred window for several seconds, then closed her eyes and groaned. It froze me to hear it.

"As soon as I saw them," she continued, "the cicadas stopped. The wind stopped, too: it was completely silent. They came toward me. I tried to run, but I couldn't move. They came closer and closer, and when I told them to leave me alone, not to touch me, they just laughed."

She looked away, a palm held flat to her forehead as if to crush the thought; then, with a visible effort, she went on.

"Each one grabbed me by an arm, and they pulled me with them. There was an old mattress on the ground outside the shack, and they were taking me toward it. I was terrified. I remember the ground there was muddy, and I said *no*, I couldn't go, I wasn't allowed to get my shoes muddy. They laughed again, and they started to drag me."

I was riveted, too horrified to utter a word.

"Black beetles swarmed out of the stuffing where a spring had broken through. I screamed and tried to run, but they caught me and I couldn't break free. One of them spun me around by the shoulders. His face was only an inch from mine, all twisted up. Even his eyes were dirty, yellowed. He stank . . ."

At that instant, Hannah was hardly aware of me. She shook her head, trying to get some distance, to step away from the two gray men decaying in their ragged clothes.

"My God, Hannah," I breathed, feeling cold and sick. "What happened?"

"I can't remember, Nick." She shrugged and tried to smile, her eyes filling. "I've tried and tried, but there's a blank I can't fill in. The next thing I knew, I was sitting on the mattress. My clothes were heaped in a pile next to me. There was no one there. The two men were gone, and the wind was moving in the trees again."

She paused, and I waited. I knew she wasn't finished yet.

"I don't know what happened," she repeated, her voice

breaking. "Maybe I dreamed the entire thing. But it seemed so *real.* I just sat there, too afraid and confused to move. I saw my footprints in the mud, the prints of my shoes, and the marks where they started to drag me. But there were only *my* prints. There should've been three sets of tracks in the mud, but there were only mine . . ."

She buried her face in her hands, exhaling a jagged, cutting sigh. Her hair fell forward, and the next instant she broke into tears, terrible to hear. Without thinking, I pushed back my chair, stepped around the table, and dropped to my knees to hold her. A trembling moved across her shoulders, and I could smell the grief on her, the sweat and fear. After a moment, her shaking stopped; her arms circled me then, returning my embrace, and she pushed her nose into my chest like a burrowing animal hunting for warmth.

She was drowning, clutching at a hand to save herself, trying to drive away the awful, numbing chill of that half-remembered afternoon. It had nothing to do with me. Even at the time, I knew that, but when she tightened her arms around me and I felt her mouth at my neck, something broke in me, broke in both of us.

I stood, lifted her off the floor in a bear hug, and walked her toward the bedroom. At the open door, she wriggled out of my embrace and turned her back to me, bracing her arms against the door jamb.

"Nick, no," she choked out, barely audible, her voice thick. "Please, we can't..."

That was Hannah's last attempt, desperate and too late, to stop what we were about to do, to keep me from taking her to the bed where she slept with another man. But I had waited too long, had caught the perfume on her skin and seen her eyes lift briefly to mine passing in the hall for too many days, to be turned aside now. I had run out of selfless gestures.

She locked her elbows, pushing against the doorjamb. My right hand skimmed down over her belly, opened the top button of her cutoffs, and slipped inside. Touching her, I glanced over her shoulder and saw the two of us in the dresser mirror on the far wall of her darkened bedroom—her expression absorbed, eyes shut, lips parted, the fine golden-brown hair falling in a veil across her face. For that instant, at least, she was mine.

"Nick," she breathed. "Hurry."

I drew the cutoffs and panties down to a pool around her ankles, pausing briefly to run my hand once between her legs. Then I stood and pushed into her. Rocking her in a circular motion, one arm locked around her waist, I watched our awkward dance, our struggle, in the mirror. Hannah looked up as her body began to tense, and when she came, our eyes met in the glass. Feeling her contract, I spilled into her at once.

We were silent for a moment; then she pulled away, kicked her clothes aside, and turned to me to be held.

What had happened was not intended, not planned by either of us, and to me, it was sweeter by far for that reason. How could it be over between us, I asked myself, when something like this could carry us off so unexpectedly? She may've only been trying to drive the death from her mind, but I didn't care. I felt her breath gradually slowing, caught the warm, earthy smell of her hair. I was exultant. After a while, Hannah lifted her face from my chest and laid a hand on my cheek, gazing up at me intently with her dark brown eyes.

"Oh God, Nick," she sighed. "What have we done?"

Her voice was heavy with regret, but her eyes were bright.

Then a car door slammed at the side of the house.

Hannah pulled frantically away and dodged off, swiping her clothes from the floor. I stood my ground, motionless in the face of her guilty panic. *The hell with it*, I thought. *Let him find us*. But when Hannah, pulling on her cutoffs, looked up at me with a pleading expression, I took up a quick position at the sink, making a show of doing the dishes. I caught her scent on my hands; behind me, I heard the brush crackling through her hair in the bedroom.

Travis walked past the streaked bay window, his arms loaded with bags, and banged in through the kitchen door, the screen slamming shut behind him. Our betrayal hung like bitter smoke in the air, impossible to ignore; but if Travis noticed, he didn't show it.

"Nick," he said, spotting me at the sink, "help me with the stuff in the car, will you?" His glance rested on me, I thought, a moment too long. His hair was wet, darkened from the rain, and for an instant I thought of my dream. He laid his bags of supplies on the table.

"Sure." I turned off the tap, drying my hands on a dish towel.

Outside, Travis said nothing. He handed bags out from the back seat of his Land Rover as the sky rumbled and another squall line blew in from the sea.

RAIN FELL FOR TWO DAYS, trapping us inside, erasing the daylight for hours at a time. Often, during the day, there was nothing for me to do but pace the rooms and brood. But the evenings were the worst. Hannah's shotgun bungalow wasn't big enough to contain three restless, guarded adults and a baffled child. Passing in the narrow hall, Hannah and I would touch without meaning to, our hands straying briefly before we caught ourselves. I was constantly on the verge of telling Travis what had happened, of having it out; but every time I was about to speak, I'd feel Hannah's gaze on me, imploring me to keep silent.

So I did. And the entire time, the house next door, not empty, loomed over us, a threat we all felt but didn't know how to confront.

Just after nightfall on the second day, the three of us sat in the parlor, listening to the steady drumming of rain on the roof. A single lamp spilled its yellow light across the floor. Each of us sat apart from the other two, not speaking, deliberately avoiding eye contact. The air was thick with intrigue and unspoken recriminations: I felt like I was choking. We were like strangers sitting in a hospital waiting room, hands clasped, eyes on the floor, dreading the news that was coming. Finally, I forced myself to speak.

"Travis," I began, turning toward his profile, "we need to talk—"

A high, shrill scream sounded from behind the house, and we all knew at once that it was Ruby. In our self-absorption, we hadn't noticed her leave.

Hannah broke and ran, and Travis and I, exchanging glances, hurried after her down the hall. We slammed through the back door into the night, the sudden darkness streaked with rain. The familiar objects of the backyard—the hedges of oleander, the spires of the iron fence—were little more than blurred, dripping shapes, shadows darker than the ashy, lightless sky. Frantic, Hannah scanned the dark, the rain plastering her hair to her face, as Travis stepped away to our right. A quick burst of lightning showed him moving deliberately through the gate, his shoulders hunched against the downpour. Then he disappeared behind the wall of oleander.

Instinctively, Hannah and I rushed after him. We found him kneeling in the grass at the base of the huge magnolia in his yard, Ruby standing rigidly beside him, his arm around her. Both of them seemed frozen in place, their eyes locked on the trunk of the tree. It took me a moment to grasp what they were seeing.

It was a cat, a neighborhood stray, the gray tiger we'd all seen slinking around the house. Someone had nailed it to the tree. Bending closer, I saw two nails penetrating the cat's chest, one through its throat, one nail driven directly into its brain. From each nail flowed a dark ribbon of blood. The animal's yellow eyes were open, its mouth stretched into a silent howl, two rows of needle-sharp teeth exposed.

Travis grasped Ruby firmly by the shoulders and turned her toward him, away from the crucified animal.

"Oh no. *God* no," Hannah muttered behind me, disbelieving, when she understood what her eyes had shown her. "Come here, baby," she coaxed, kneeling, and Ruby threw herself sobbing into her mother's arms.

Travis rose from his knees, Hannah lifted Ruby and stood, and the three of us regarded each other in silence. Rain splattered on the broad leaves of the magnolia. Then, without warning, before any of us could form a sane response or find the words to convey it, a white rectangle was stamped like a tattoo over the wet black lawn at our feet. Even in the dark, I could see the outrage—the weeks of fear and balked anger—working on Travis's face as he turned up into the rain to glare at the house. A light had been switched on in an upstairs room. I glanced up in time to see the old man's face and shoulders, in profile, slide out of the lighted frame.

Travis had taken a single step toward the back door, fists clenched, his gaze locked on that glowing window, when Hannah reached out to stop him.

"What do you think *you're* doing?" she demanded, shifting Ruby in her arms as she confronted him. "You can't mean to go in there!"

He turned to face her. Even in the dark, you could see the thought turning in his eyes.

Then he grabbed her by the arm and led her firmly to where I stood a few feet away, watching.

"*Here*," he said, looking at me steadily, fixedly, to be sure I understood. "You want her. Take her!"

So he knew. Hannah glanced at me, too shocked to respond. "Keep her safe, Nick," he added.

Turning on his heels, Travis strode toward the back door,

rummaging in one pocket for the key. I'd made a move to follow him when Hannah stopped me.

"*Let him go!*" she pleaded. Ruby clung, silent, to her mother's neck, and Hannah looked past the child's rain-slicked head to hold me with her eyes. "Stay with us. *Please*, Nick. You can't help him."

At the time, with her hand on my arm and her dark eyes probing mine, it was an easy decision to make. Standing for a moment longer in that relentless, stinging rain, I turned to watch him unlock the door, slip into the black kitchen, and vanish.

VII

THE NEXT MORNING, I woke to sunlight slanting into Hannah's room through the blinds, laying bright, clean stripes across her bed and floor. Hannah slept facing the wall, as she always used to, her right knee raised. Some time during the night, Ruby had crept into bed between us and dozed now curled against her mother's back. For a moment, I felt at peace, as if the last seven weeks had dissolved in the fresh clarity of the morning air and nothing had happened to undermine my contentment. But then I remembered Travis, saw him step alone into that terrible house, and it was like tumbling out of paradise into a world of complicity and guilt. I sat up at once and swung my legs to the floor.

Feeling me stir, Hannah turned over groggily. "Where are you going?" she asked. Next to her, Ruby whined in her sleep, impatient at being disturbed.

"I need to find Travis," I told her. "He never came back last night."

Suddenly awake, she pushed the hair out of her eyes and sat up to regard me. She started to speak, but I put a hand on her arm. "Don't worry. I'll be right back," I assured her. "Lock the door after me. I just want to make sure he's all right."

So I threw some water in my face, re-tied my unraveling ponytail, dressed, and headed next door. The storm doors were bolted in front, but the back, where he'd entered the house the night before, was still unlocked. As I stepped tentatively over the threshold, I felt like an intruder, and the sound of my boots on the hardwood floors seemed loud in the silence.

The downstairs rooms were empty, as I'd expected, so I started up the creaky, step-worn stairs, calling out so I wouldn't alarm him.

"Travis! It's me! It's Nick! Are you in here?"

There was no response. The sound of my own voice was comforting in the ponderous stillness of the house. I paused at the top of the landing, hand on the banister, and called out again.

No answer.

Tapping with one knuckle at his hammer-scarred bedroom door, I opened it to find the room deserted in the morning sunlight, the bed made, the shadows of live oaks stirring across the freshly painted walls in the breeze. From the look of the room and the murmuring of doves trailing in through the open window, no one would ever have guessed that anything sinister had happened there. One by one, I walked through the vacant upstairs rooms, my steps the only sound. I was telling myself that Travis was angry, as I had been, that he'd left the island or taken a motel room on the seawall. Then, going through the rounds, I swung open the heavy oak door of the turret room and found myself confronted by two staring eyes.

Travis sat on the floor with his back against the wall. A thin trail of blood, dried now, ran from the nail driven into his forehead. He stared at me as if he were about to speak.

I backed out of the room, reaching instinctively for the cell phone clipped to my belt. Stumbling down the stairs, I dialed 9-1-1. I needed to get out of that house, out of the shadows.

Unlatching the storm doors, I threw them open and collapsed on the front steps, cold with sweat, and waited for the ambulance to arrive.

I felt removed from myself, absent, as if I'd been lifted out of my body. Blankly, I watched the light falling through the trees to shift in patterns over the street. In an upstairs room, my friend was dead. When the ambulance arrived, siren blaring and the red light spinning crazily on the roof, I sat on the steps impassively looking on, as if I were watching the film of someone else's life. Attempting to shake off the heavy spell, I stood to approach the paramedics, nearly blacked out, and had to sit again. Then two plainclothes cops screeched up in an unmarked Ford. I pulled myself together and told them what I'd found.

Hannah and Ruby, drawn by the commotion and flashing lights, came over just in time to see Travis's body, zipped into a black plastic bag, being carried down the front stairs on a gurney. Hannah put a hand over her mouth and stared; she went pale as bone through her suntan, the tears standing in her eyes. Meaning to help, Ruby told the detectives about the man with a hammer. I confirmed seeing him around the house, gave them a description, and led them to the cat we'd found nailed to the trunk of the magnolia out back.

And so, that same crystal morning, with the first trace of fall in the air, the cops dusted the nails for prints and started looking for a suspect they'd never find.

THE SERVICE WAS HELD at the Eisenhardt Funeral Home on Broadway. Hannah, Ruby, and I sat on folding metal chairs in a small carpeted room with the closed casket. Arrangements had been made to ship Travis's body to his parents in the Hill Country later that day. He'd known almost no one on the island, and the only other person who came was the old woman who lived across the street, Dolly McCaslin, with whom Travis had discussed recipes for lemon pound cake one hot afternoon in July. She stood in the back of the room, looking vaguely lost in her floral dress and white gloves, until Hannah noticed her and showed her to a seat.

Afterward, Hannah dropped Ruby off at school and went reluctantly to work. There was really nothing to do but try to get on with our lives.

Left on my own, I sat on the back steps of Travis's house, elbows on my knees, remembering. The things he'd said to me there in the twilight tumbled through my mind. I'd only known Travis Karlson for a few weeks, hardly long enough to know who someone truly is, but his words had opened doors and changed the world for me. I felt guilty—terribly, crushingly guilty—for letting him go into that house alone. But I knew very well, even then, that faced with the same decision I would make exactly the same choice. I thought of that dark old man stalking the property, guarding his secret, and how his grandson as a boy had found him brooding over the roses at night. A fragment of a dream I'd forgotten spun up in my mind: Ruby holding a rosebud; it opened, petal by petal, and a face appeared in the center of the flower, the eyes rolling open like an antique doll's . . .

Instantly, I sat up straight, riveted. I knew at once what I had to do. The roses along the back fence shook in a sudden breeze.

The old shovel Travis had used still leaned against the back of the house. I clutched its grip-smoothed wooden handle and crossed the yard. In no time at all, I'd shoveled out the mulch that he'd piled around the rosebushes. A moment more, and I hit older dirt.

Then I found her. Somehow, I knew at once that it was a woman. I leaned on the shovel, looking down at the delicate, earth-stained curve of a scapula. Travis's twisted, malignant grandfather must've worried, every time it rained, that his secret would break through to the light. Still, I think he liked her near, close to the surface, available. Travis and I had stared out at those flowers, watching them darken gradually in the twilight, and we'd never known what was hidden in them, what they meant.

I knew I had to call the police; but first, I needed to know exactly how it had happened, something the cops would never be able to tell me. But I knew who would. Bobbi was home when I called her, and in twenty minutes her faded, salt-stained Honda Civic pulled up in front of the house. The driver's door creaked open and Bobbi's long, angular form extracted itself awkwardly from behind the wheel.

"Thanks for coming," I told her. "I know how difficult it is for you to be here."

She nodded curtly, her features set. She had the look of someone straining to listen through a din of voices, as if she were hearing a dozen radios turned on at once. I had some inkling then of what it must've been like for her; and it was worse, I'm sure, in the East End. I led her out back, and the two of us stood looking down at the bones in the roses. For a long time, Bobbi was silent. Then the wind fumbled through the stand of oleanders and she sighed, seeming to come back to herself.

"Jesus Christ," was all she said. She turned anxiously to glance at the house behind us.

"Take me to my car, Nickie."

Standing at the open door of her Honda, eager to make her escape, Bobbi told me what she knew. As she spoke, her eyes flicked continually past my shoulder to the house.

"They were caught on the second floor, just the two of them. The water was rising."

"During the storm, you mean?"

Bobbi nodded impatiently. "Of course. Looking out the windows, they saw bodies, dozens of them, floating past in the tide. He thought they were going to die, that he wouldn't have to answer for what he did, so he dragged her by the hair into a room.

That room," she added, pointing past me to the turret room, the room where I'd found Travis. It was washed in shade at the far corner of the house. "He raped her. It went on for hours, and when the water began to fall and he knew they wouldn't drown, he couldn't let her live. She begged for her life, but things had gone too far. He stunned her with the hammer. Then he held her head steady between his knees and drove a nail into her skull, and then another one, just to be sure." A hand rose to cover her eyes. After a moment it fell, and Bobbi glared at me with a raw expression, a single tear trailing disregarded down her haggard face. "He *did* things with the body. Things he liked. Things he could never forget. He kept her for two days, and then he buried her behind the house."

"You mean to tell me no one saw?"

She pinned me with her eyes. "There were so many dead, Nickie. So many. Nobody noticed an extra corpse."

I turned to survey the street, the flowing shade of the hundred-year-old live oaks, the carved gables with their hand-blown windows jutting above the trees, suddenly reminded that I lived in a graveyard. At that moment, the branches forming a tunnel over the road looked like the entrance to the underworld.

"*Shovel the dirt back in!*" Bobbi urged me suddenly, and I swung back to face her. "That thing in the house, that horrible old man—he knows who you are! Do you understand what I'm telling you? He'll come looking for you."

I called up the sullen face turning to me in the twilight at the front gate, showing itself just long enough to create terror, the hatred coming off of him like white noise. *Let him come*, I thought. Travis had been determined to uncover the old man's secret. Now it was up to me to finish the job. I owed him that much.

Bobbi must've seen the answer on my face. Exasperated, she poured herself into her car, slammed the door, and turned over the engine. But before she pulled away, she lowered the window and leaned out to confront me

"Then at least get off the island," she insisted. "And take that woman and her little girl with you. Don't be a goddamn fool, Nickie. Do you think you can protect yourself any better than your friend could?"

Bobbi roared off down the street, distracted by the whispering and pleading of the dead, angry and afraid because she didn't want to see me get hurt, and anxious, I knew, to escape the shadows and get out on the safer, more open stretches of beach, where nothing could approach without being seen.

I called the cops then. I'd found bones in the backyard, I told them. Yes, I believed they were human. Would they please hurry?

The police cordoned off the area with yellow tape and soon found the rest of the bones and removed them. They took a brief statement from me and left. But the next day, after the coroner had found the holes driven through the skull, they brought me in for more questioning. A neighbor had informed them about the rivalry between Travis and me, so they already suspected me in Travis's death—though Hannah had confirmed that I was with her all night and there was no forensic evidence tying me to the scene. I'm sure they must've thought that the two deaths were related; and they were, of course, but in a manner the police would've found it impossible to believe. A few days later, I was cleared when the forensics team discovered that the bones and fragments of clothing they'd collected were a hundred years old. The murder had been committed before I was born.

Then they found a partial print on the nail driven into Travis's brain. It gave me a chill when I heard that, but there was no point in trying to tell them that they'd found a dead man's thumbprint. Anyway, the print wasn't mine, and it got me off the hook for good.

Sitting in the sunlight at Hannah's kitchen table one morning, we read in the paper that the name of the woman in the roses was Flora. That name and the name of her husband, James, had been engraved along with the date of their wedding on the inside of the ring still circling the bone of her finger. Seeing the word in print, it came to me: her name was her fate. She'd become flowers.

After everything that had happened, it wasn't difficult to convince Hannah that we had to leave the island. She was a little concerned about taking Ruby out of class so far into the school year, but she knew as well as I did that her daughter could finish first grade elsewhere, hopefully some place with fewer bad memories. Keeping a close eye on the two of them, I did what had to be done as quickly as I could, putting my bungalow up for sale and making a few improvements to Hannah's place, installing new cabinets in the kitchen and a whirlpool tub in the bath, before she put her house on the market, as well.

One dank, foggy morning in the second week of October, we backed out of Hannah's driveway, Ruby on the seat between us, and left the island for good. The few pieces of furniture we were taking with us were tied down under tarps in the flatbed of my truck. Strangely, despite everything, I felt an ache of regret. Galveston had been my home, and I knew better than anyone that we could never come back. Crossing the bridge over the bay, my eyes flicked continually to the rearview mirror, but there was nothing to see. The low profile of the island with its old trees and houses had been swallowed in the thick wall of white mist rolling in off the Gulf.

We drove for nearly fifteen hours straight, arriving at her parents' farm in Missouri, and there, on October 28, on one of those warm, mellow autumn days that feels deceptively like spring, Hannah and I were married in their backyard. Ruby was our flower girl, the ceremony attended by a handful of neighbors and a few old friends of Hannah's from high school. Fanning out beyond the yard with its rented floral arbor, the ditches on her father's land were crammed with sunflowers turning their blind faces to the light. For both of us, getting married was an act of faith in a future we needed to believe in.

And there was another reason: Hannah was pregnant. In her pumpkin-colored dress and wreath of baby's breath, she wasn't showing her condition that day. But I knew. What I didn't know, and what Hannah couldn't tell me, was whether the child was Travis's or mine.

We stayed in Missouri through Thanksgiving, the three of us taking long walks with her parents when the weather was good. Rabbits exploded from the underbrush, showing us the white flare of their tails as they vanished. There was a palpable sense of pause, a feeling of waiting for the next thing to happen, but Hannah and I both knew that it couldn't happen there. I had a former customer whose house I'd restored in Galveston; he spent the winters on the island and lived the rest of the year in one of Frank Lloyd Wright's prairie homes in Oak Park, Illinois. For some time, he'd been after me to come north and work on his place, assuring me that he could get me certified to do so. I decided to take him up on his offer—it felt like a safe distance from the Gulf of Mexico.

Hannah, Ruby, and I arrived in Illinois at the same time that winter did. We were Southerners, used to warm Gulf breezes, and the bitter, biting cold that swept down from Canada to linger over the flat stretches of prairie came as a shock to us. Our places in Galveston had sold by then, and we bought a white clapboard farmhouse, just west of Aurora, with wooden floors, three bedrooms, beamed ceilings, a brick fireplace, and a wide front porch. A foot of snow fell and didn't melt, and in a week, it snowed again. While Hannah slept in the afternoons, I began, in a drafty upstairs room at the front of the house, to write down the story of what had happened that summer, connecting the fragments, trying to sort out the tale by telling it. I needed to give a clear account of Travis, who could no longer speak for himself.

When that first harsh grip of winter relaxed a bit, I was able to get to Oak Park on a regular basis, driving east toward Chicago on the Eisenhower Expressway. Since we needed the money, I worked quickly to complete the job, and as luck would have it, my client's refurbished house was on the Oak Park historic homes tour that spring. People saw what I'd done, and I soon had more than enough work to keep me busy.

I love restoring those light-filled, hand-crafted houses; they're entirely different than the dark, vertical places I knew in the East End. Low-pitched roofs and horizontal lines reflect the wide, flat spaces of the prairie, the rooms open, lighted by rows of casement windows that run, often, the length of an entire wall. Working in some flawlessly proportioned space, refinishing the intricate pattern of a parquet floor or the perfect curve of a staircase, I imagine the brooding Master himself, dressed in black with his long, pale face, a set of blueprints under his arm, stepping through the ribs of lumber, giving final directions to his crew. The sound of saws and hammers has drawn a group of local boys, who crowd a framed, unfinished doorway to watch the work proceed. Among them, I like to think, in knickerbockers, squinting under a snap-brim cap, is a young Ernest Hemingway, who grew up in Oak Park. The boy observes carefully as the workmen fit a length of two-by-four snugly, effortlessly, to the crossbeam, getting his first lesson in craftsmanship.

MY STORY IS ALMOST finished now. From the second-floor window of my study, I can look up from the page to a rolling meadow, lush and green in the May sunlight, a reminder of the expanse of prairie that once existed here. The first daisies float above the grass like water lilies. When that stretch of green moves all at the same time in a breeze with nothing to stop it for miles, it's easy to understand how the first settlers, crossing the land in their Conestoga wagons, sometimes felt they were lost at sea.

This morning, I stepped out on the porch, coffee in hand, and looked across the field to the split-rail fence at the edge of the woods in the distance, my eyes drawn by movement there. An old man stepped out of the trees, the brim of his dark fedora pulled low across his face. For an instant, I froze and held my breath. Then the familiar Black Lab appeared, nuzzling the man's hand, and I recognized our neighbor, John Wiley. Seeing me shade my eyes to observe him, he raised an arm in greeting. After a moment the world returned, and I felt I could breathe again.

On the porch swing below me, Hannah rocks slowly and waits for her baby, her arms around her belly. She watches for Ruby's yellow school bus, waiting for it to come around the bend, as it will any minute. I'm living a borrowed life, the one that Travis lent me—doing his work, sleeping with the woman he'd chosen, and shortly, for all I know or care to know, raising as my own the child he left us. He sacrificed himself for us; whatever life we can find here we'll have because of him.

Sometimes I still dream about him. We're sitting on the back steps of his place in the East End, in a vanished world, as a slow summer twilight deepens and the crickets trill. He's drawing me into some enlarging mystery. Then he's silent, and as I watch, he turns to me. I can barely make out his face in the darkness, but then I see that he's smiling, and I know that he's okay, that everything, eventually, will be all right.

About the Author

James Ulmer received his MA from the University of Washington and his PhD from The Writing Program at the University of Houston. He served as a Literature Panelist for The Texas Commission on the Arts and has received fellowships and awards for his writing, including a Residency at The MacDowell Colony, two Cultural Arts Council of Houston Creative Artist Program Grants, two Academy of American Poets Prizes, the Pablo Neruda Prize, the PEN Southwest Discovery prize, and grants from The Ohio Arts Council and The Washington State Commission for the Humanities. A collection of poems, *Notes Toward a City of Rain*, was published in 1996. For many years, Ulmer was Writer-in-Residence at Houston Baptist University. He is currently Chair of the Department of English and Foreign Languages at Southern Arkansas University.